FORSAKEN ROAD

Book One in the Swansbane Scrolls

by S. K. Moonie

ISBN: 978-0-9756298-2-6

CONTENTS

AUTHOR COMMENTS

You know how some stories just live in your head for decades? That was 'Forsaken Road' for me.

When I finally wrote it down, which was a few years ago, I was basically transcribing a story inspired by ten years of day-long RPG sessions. In the old days it was with character sheets so yellow they could pass for ancient scrolls and hand-drawn dungeon maps with beer stains that became my literary roadmap. Nowadays the character sheets are all on Excel but I still prefer hand-drawn maps.

I've been a tabletop RPG nerd since the late 80s, and it was never the simple stuff. I tried many systems, with AD&D being the gateway of course (see NOTE). But it was Avalon Hill's 'Powers and Perils' that I fell in love with (https://powersandperils.org/). P&P is basically the gaming equivalent of calculus with a ridiculously steep learning curve... but man, the detail! 'Forsaken Road' and thence the entire Rande series grew from me trying to introduce my clueless friends to the system. You should've seen their faces when they realised what they'd signed up for!

'The Architect's Tomb' was the next adventure, followed by books 3 and 4 ('Tower of the Damned' and 'Bloodied Waters'). Books 3 & 4 were total improv adventures where the player's choices greatly influenced the outcome. Books 5, 'The Depths of Deceit' and 3, 'The Architect's Tomb', were much more mapped out for reasons that will become obvious when you read them.

What makes Rande different?

I call it "realistic fantasy" because I'm allergic to tropes of convenience. Strangers do not meet in a tavern and instantly become BFFs willing to die for each other. Adventurers take jobs because they're broke and hungry, not because looting tombs is a noble calling. And magic? It absolutely exists and it's insanely powerful, but it can be risky to use.

So, what about Rande itself? It is not some cosy fantasy playground; it's brutal, unforgiving, and couldn't care less if you live or die. Heroes might think they're the main character, but try telling that to everyone else in the story!

NOTE: My mother gave away my <u>complete</u> set of AD&D 1st edition manuals and adventures to an op-shop back in the late 90s - I have never completely forgiven her for that.

GOOD NEWS: 'The Architect's Tomb' is almost ready. The second draft is sitting on my computer and being torn apart by my editors. With any luck, Mardonius and Akantha will be back to continue the adventure before the year's out!

Join me at https://discord.gg/rxH5HY48 for discussions and up-to-date details on the battle for Swansbane series!

MAP

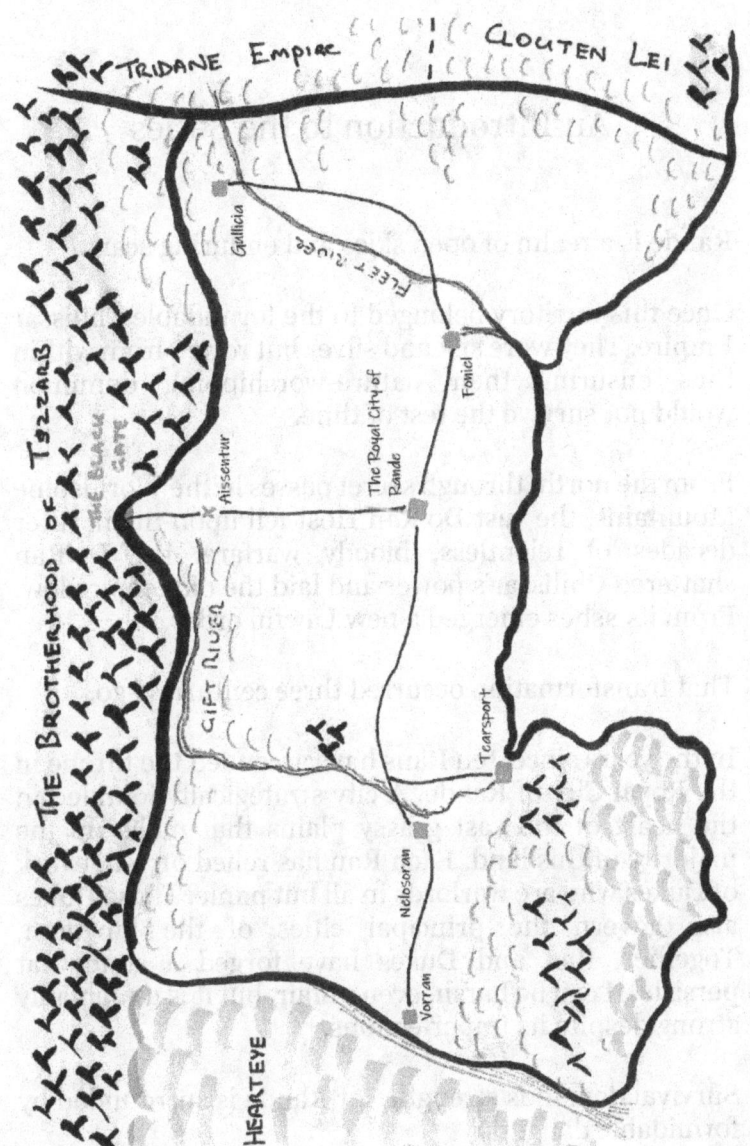

THE LEGACY OF RANDE

An Introduction to the Series

Rande is a realm of open skies and enduring scars.

Once this territory belonged to the formidable Chilissar Empire. They wore silk and silver but rotted from within thus ensuring their nature-worshipping dominion would not survive the test of time.

From the north, through secret passes in the Worldspine Mountains, the vast Do'Ran Host fell upon them. After decades of relentless, bloody warfare, the Do'Ran shattered Chilissar's power and laid the old empire low. From its ashes emerged a new Lawful order.

That transformation occurred three centuries ago.

In the years since, ten Rans have ascended the throne in the Royal City of Rande. A city strategically founded in the heart of the vast grassy plains that make up the majority of this land. Each Ran has relied on a network of Dukes who are warlords in all but name. These Dukes also govern the principal cities of the kingdom. Together, Ran and Dukes have forged a state that persists. It can be harsh, even unfair, but it is undeniably strong despite its imperfections.

Survival demands strength, for Rande is surrounded by formidable dangers.

East of its borders the faltering Tridaine Empire waits, its designs on former glory are only thinly concealed. There too is the Host of Clouten Lei, a loose alliance of tribes guided by shamans and ancient hatred. The Host is completely unpredictable but should a charismatic leader arise it could pose a grave threat.

To the south lies Hyrrack, a nation of Chaos-worshipping corsairs who strike like wolves upon the waves, spreading terror wherever their black vessels land.

Beyond high stone ramparts and frigid mountain passes to the north stands the Brotherhood of Tszzarb. An ancient alliance of Dwarves and hardened men, they now speak of peace and trade but are not yet forgiven for their last assault on Rande just thirty summers past.

In the ancient forests powers older than humankind still stir. The Fey, beautiful, lethal and utterly alien, haunt the woods as if they were spirits. Elves, Fayrie and worse, their most fearsome domain is the HeartEye, an immense forest stretching across the entire western border. Many humans have sought to pillage the wealth of this vast forest but none are known to have returned.

And yet, with all this, Rande endures. Its people, the Randeri, uphold Law and tradition with steadfast devotion. Most venerate Eanna, the Warrior Goddess, Lady of Resplendent Light, under whose name justice is swift and as fair as can be. A strand of brutal ruthlessness still runs through the nobility, a legacy of the Do'Ran Host that has not fully faded. For commoners, existence is stable but rarely easy.

Rande may be harsh, but it offers a rare gift: opportunity.

The territory is rich. Its fields feed armies and cities with enough surplus for export. Rande Dark Ore, quarried from deep veins and an easy host for powerful magic, commands a high price across the known world. Timber known as Feywood, harvested at immense risk from only the most ancient of woods, yields the finest furniture, ships and bows. Game roams the plains in abundance and gold still glitters among the ruins of long-vanished monarchs.

This is a realm where fortunes are made, legends are born, and power awaits those bold enough to claim it.

PROLOGUE

4 days earlier.

Mardonius gasped, each laboured breath scorching his lungs as he forced his way through the tangled alleys of Old Rande's lowest district. Early spring had arrived, the noonday sun hammered down without mercy, turning every narrow passage into a furnace of stink and sound. He pressed his back against a grimy wall, seeking a momentary reprieve from the heat and the chase.

Around him the alleys constricted like the intestines of some colossal creature, their leaning walls so close that opposing balconies almost met overhead. A thin ribbon of sky, visible between them, felt like freedom just out of reach. Mardonius wondered whether these ancient buildings had already stood when the Chilissar Empire fell three centuries ago.

Sweat slid down his spine, soaking the thin civilian tunic that seemed absurdly fragile compared with the leather armour he had worn for a decade of service. He ducked under a clothesline heavy with faded sheets and tunics. Despite the urgency of his flight each step remained measured, a habit forged through ten years of drilling. Yet, where training once demanded he stand tall, he now hunched his shoulders, shrinking into himself to avoid drawing attention.

A piercing laugh erupted from a nearby doorway as two children darted out, nearly colliding with his legs. Mardonius twisted on his heel hand instinctively reaching for a weapon that was not there. The children scattered, oblivious to his presence.

"Fresh eels! From the northern lakes!" called a vendor, the cry slicing through the clamour and followed by the jangle of a pot lid. The metallic clang jolted Mardonius as sharply as a camp's alarm bell.

Every sense quivered beneath the onslaught of noise: the butcher's rhythmic chopping, the heated haggling at a cloth merchant's stall, the distant wail of an infant. He strained to pick out the cadence of boots on cobbles and the distinctive clink of military-issue gear, any sound that might signal Licarin's men closing in on his trail.

Turning down an even narrower passage, the stench nearly bowled him over. Urine and rotting vegetables fermented in the gutter mingling with the coppery tang of blood from a nearby slaughterhouse. By contrast the sweet smell of freshly baked rolls from a bakery smelled cloying and sickening. Over it all hung the unmistakable odour of too many unwashed bodies crammed into too little space.

His fingers strayed to the coin pouch at his belt. It was flat and nearly empty. Two coppers and seven brass bits. After ten years of loyal service to the Ran he had been promised enough gold to begin a new life. Now he might be forced to trade everything away just for the chance to see tomorrow's dawn.

That morning already felt like a lifetime ago, though the sun had climbed no higher than halfway across the sky.

At dawn he'd risen with hope in his step, meticulously cleaning his few civilian clothes and practising the respectful words he would speak to the quartermasters who processed his demobilisation. He'd imagined that by sunset he would finally hold five gleaming gold coins as payment for long service.

A mangy dog snarled from a doorway, ribs jutting through dirty fur. Mardonius skirted around it. He was well aware that animals sensed fear and that his fear throbbed in time with his pulse.

Adrenaline from his frantic flight began to ebb, leaving his limbs heavy and unsteady. A cut on his forearm throbbed from a glancing blow. Every breath reminded him of forced marches and hunger; hardships he had endured easily when purpose and comrades stood at his side. Now he had only himself, hunted by a vendetta-driven officer with nearly unlimited resources at his disposal.

His shoulder scraped rough timber as he squeezed through a gap just wide enough for a man. Fear and rage fought for control, but his anger was reserved for Flag-Commander Licarin rather than the hired blades who had tried to kill him, they were just pawns.

At last he spotted a recessed doorway cloaked in shadow and let himself slide down to a crouch, back to the wall. Every muscle trembled with exhaustion. He closed his eyes for three conscious breaths; control the breathing, control the pain. He then began cataloguing his surroundings with the intense focus of a seasoned unit leader. The passage connected two larger thoroughfares. Three and four-storey buildings leaned so far over that they nearly blotted out the sky. No sign of military patrols. Enough civilians moving about that any struggle would draw unwelcome attention.

He massaged a tender bruise on his calf whose cause he could not even remember. His ribs protested from impact with a stone bench during his escape. His throat was parched from thirst and the smoky city air.

Exactly seventeen breaths later, counted out as he would in the heat of battle, he pushed himself upright. Ignoring the protest of overworked muscles, he slipped back into the chaotic flow of Rande's underbelly, determined to become a single anonymous drop in a river of humanity.

Earlier that morning, Mardonius had approached the Eastern Legion headquarters with the same deliberate precision he'd once used to advance on enemy positions. The sun had barely crested the city walls. It painted the white stone of the barracks a deceptive rose-gold. He'd polished his boots, civilian leather not military issue, and combed his hair with water to flatten the soldier's crop he was trying to grow out.

The Training Headquarters for the Eastern Legion dominated the north-eastern quarter of Rande, its walls rising twice as high as the surrounding buildings. The Royal Army's blue pennants hung limp in the still morning air, each emblazoned with the same silver star that adorned Mardonius' shield. He'd covered the shield and its star with a hand-stitched leather cover when he left his unit, not all who knew of the Royal Army loved it, so as a civilian he felt there was no sense advertising his past. Seeing the familiar insignia still sent a pulse of pride through him though.

A queue of hopeful recruits had already formed outside the main entrance. They were farmers and townspeople, predominantly men but also a couple of women, their faces a mixture of trepidation and forced bravado.

Mardonius skirted them, heading instead to the veterans' entrance at the eastern side of the compound. Ten years ago, he'd stood in that same recruit line. 16 years old with his rural accent still thick on his tongue and calluses on his hands from felling trees rather than drawing a bowstring.

"State your business," the gate guard demanded, his uniform crisp despite the early hour. Though the man was young, perhaps twenty, his posture betrayed the rigid discipline of the Eastern Legion. His hand rested easily on his ceremonial spear, but his eyes performed the automatic threat assessment that became second nature to any soldier who survived their initial campaign.

"Mardonius, Wagon Master, North-eastern Company. Here to finalise discharge and collect demobilisation payment." Mardonius held up the metal token stamped with his name, details and term of service. Handing this over would signal the end of his duty.

The guard's eyebrows lifted slightly at "Wagon Master", a leader of 80 men. The rank was earned through merit, not birth, and spoke of significant battlefield experience. He examined the token with renewed interest before returning it with a fraction more respect than before.

"Administration building, third courtyard. Quartermasters will be receiving veterans after the morning bell." He stepped aside, bringing his fist to his chest in the Legion's salute. Mardonius return the gesture instinctively, a habit formed through thousands of repetitions.

The compound stretched before him, painfully familiar. The whitewashed stone buildings arranged in perfect squares. The parade grounds where he'd spent countless hours drilling recruits. The archery range where he'd earned the notice of his first commander. Everywhere, soldiers moved with purpose; a column of spearmen marching to morning exercise, messengers darting between buildings, servants carrying breakfast to the officers' quarters.

He walked the familiar paths, his body remembering the rhythm of this place even as his mind catalogued the changes from his last posting here. New target dummies on the archery range. A fresh coat of paint on the officers' quarters. A different arrangement of the outdoor mess tables. Small changes that made the immutable nature of military life all the more apparent.

In the third courtyard, several benches had been positioned against the administration building's wall. Three men already waited, each bearing the indefinable mark of a veteran in the way they sat, alert even in repose, eyes constantly sweeping their surroundings. One wore a leather patch where his left eye should have been. Another had hands so gnarled with old breaks they resembled twisted tree roots more than human appendages. The third, youngest of the group, wore his uniform pants with one leg pinned up neatly at the knee.

Mardonius bowed his head to them, receiving their acknowledgments in return. The unspoken brotherhood of men who had survived what others hadn't. He chose a bench slightly apart from them, his back to the wall, with clear sightlines to both entrances to the courtyard. It was a habit he'd developed in border taverns where Randeri soldiers were rarely welcome.

As the sun climbed higher, the courtyard filled with the sounds of a waking military post. Tent Masters shouting cadence. Steel ringing against steel from the practice yard. The smells were just as familiar. There was the scent oil used for weapons maintenance and the particular soap the Quartermaster issued that never quite removed the smell of sweat.

Five gold coins, equivalent to 50 silvers or 500 coppers! Enough to buy a small holding in one of the northern provinces, far from the east and its memories. Enough for land, seed, perhaps even a milk cow if he was frugal. He'd build the cabin himself, his hands remembered how to shape wood into shelter, a skill from childhood reinforced by military necessity. By summer, he'd have a roof and walls of his own. By the next spring, the first crops. It wasn't glory or wealth, but it would be his, earned through blood and loyalty.

The administration building's doors opened precisely at the second bell. A clerk emerged wearing a disinterested expression and carrying a stack of parchment. He was a thin man who looked for all the world like a stick wearing the uniform tunic.

"Veterans for discharge processing. Form a line and have your documentation ready," he called, his voice reedy and uncaring.

Mardonius waited for the others to rise, a courtesy to the wounded, before taking his place in line. The clerk examined each man's token, checking names against his list, directing them to different offices within. When Mardonius' turn came, the clerk's eyes narrowed slightly.

"North-eastern Company?" he asked, voice carefully neutral.

"Yes. Under March Commander Elbren for seven years, then Flag Commander Licarin for three." Mardonius kept his tone equally non-committal.

The clerk made a mark on his parchment. "Wait here. Your paperwork requires special authorisation."

Something in the clerk's avoidance of eye contact sent a whisper of warning through Mardonius' mind, but he simply stepped aside. The morning stretched on. The other veterans emerged one by one, some clutching small pouches that clinked with the weight of their due payment, others with resignation on their faces as they were told to return another day. Still, Mardonius waited, watching the sun climb higher, feeling the first stirrings of unease crawl along his spine.

He knew the moment his name reached Licarin's desk. Knew without seeing that somewhere in this vast complex of military bureaucracy, a man who had respected him for years was instead now plotting against him. Yet he waited, clinging to procedure, to the hope that ten years of service still meant something.

A junior clerk finally emerged from the administration building, his face an expressionless mask. "Wagon Master Mardonius? Your paperwork is being processed in the northern office. You'll need to cross the training ground to reach it." The words were ordinary enough, but something in the way the clerk's eyes avoided his own only heightened his concern.

"Northern office?" Mardonius repeated, buying seconds while his mind raced. Discharge processing had always been handled in the central administration building.

Ten years in the Army had taught him the rigid pathways of military bureaucracy; changes to procedure were unthinkable.

The clerk merely turned away, a puppet whose role was completed. Mardonius watched him go, then squared his shoulders and walked through the archway leading to the main training yard. Every instinct urged caution, yet turning back now would only draw attention. Better to appear the unsuspecting fool and keep his senses sharp.

The training ground stretched before him, an expanse of hard-packed dirt surrounded by the grey stone barracks. In ordinary times, the yard would be crowded with drilling soldiers engaged in formation marches, weapons practice and hand-to-hand combat training. Today, it was empty save for three men in recruit tunics training with wooden maces near the far edge.

Mardonius kept his pace steady and relaxed but his mind catalogued every detail. The so-called recruits moved with a fluidity that spoke of years of combat experience. Their footwork was too precise, their balance too perfect. A true recruit's movements were hesitant thanks to muscles still learning the unnatural positions of formal combat. These men had the confident economy of motion that only came from having used those skills to stay alive.

Halfway across the yard, the hairs on the back of his neck rose. He'd angled his path to give the sparring men a wide berth but they adjusted their positions, spreading out in a formation that would intercept him before he reached the northern building. Casual observers might see nothing unusual, just training exercises moving across the yard, but Mardonius recognised the tactical positioning and the way they maintained awareness of each other even while pretending to focus on their stance and balance.

The sunlight caught on one man's weapon as he swung it in a controlled arc and Mardonius' suspicions crystallised into certainty. The maces used by recruits were solid wood. They were designed to teach proper form without causing fatal injury. But these had been modified with metal bands wrapped around the heads and small but vicious spikes added to what should have been smooth surfaces. One solid blow from such a weapon would shatter bone. A strike to the head could be instantly fatal.

Mardonius' pace didn't falter but his mind raced through scenarios with the rapid calculations that had become second nature. Three visible opponents. Unknown numbers inside the northern building. No weapons of his own. He'd left everything at the inn; arriving armed for a routine administrative matter would have been a breach of protocol. The main gate lay fifty paces behind him. There were two smaller side exits, both likely watched.

A flutter of movement from above caught his attention. Mardonius allowed his attention to drift upward, careful not to betray his focus. A window on the second floor of the northern building stood open, and in it, a figure watched the unfolding scene with the stillness of a predator.

Even at this distance, Flag Commander Licarin Fie'Zu'Ran was unmistakable. The distinctive dark blue cloak with silver trim marked his rank, but Mardonius would have known him regardless. The commander's tall, gaunt frame seemed to consume light rather than reflect it. His prematurely greyed hair was cropped close to his skull in the military style that serving nobles favoured. But it was his stillness that identified him most clearly, Licarin had always possessed the unnerving ability to remain perfectly motionless, like a snake before it strikes.

Their eyes met across the distance and Mardonius felt a cold weight settle in his stomach. There was no shock in Licarin's gaze, no hesitation, just the cold certainty of a man who has given an order and expects to see it fulfilled. This was no misunderstanding, no bureaucratic error, this was to be a calculated execution.

The memory of Daffir Fie'Zu'Ran flashed through Mardonius' mind, the commander's son, barely twenty, assigned to Mardonius' Wagon for 3 years. During what should have been a routine supply mission to the northern outposts an ambush had evaded the flanking Randeri spearmen. With surprise on their side, the enemy, perverted creatures known as 'The Twisted' hit Mardonius' archers hard. Six men lost out of 80, including young Daffir, despite Mardonius' best efforts to save them all. A trumped up official inquiry had cleared him of wrongdoing. He'd followed protocol, taken appropriate precautions and if anything it was the spearmen who failed, but a father's grief cared not for facts. With just a few months left to serve this incident had now come back to haunt him.

Mardonius understood vengeance. In another life, he might even have respected Licarin's dedication to avenging his son. But understanding didn't mean submission. He hadn't survived a decade of border skirmishes and pitched battles to die unarmed in a training yard, killed by men who brought lethal weapons to what should have been a place of learning.

He was three-quarters of the way across the yard now. The disguised killers had stopped pretending to train, their positions began forming a loose semicircle that would close around him in moments. Behind them, the door to the northern building remained closed. There were to be no accidental witnesses or interruptions in what would be dismissed as a training accident: a discharged veteran who unwisely interfered in recruit exercises.

Mardonius made his decision in the fraction of a heartbeat that separated life from death on any battlefield. He stopped abruptly, as if only just noticing something amiss, turned on his heel and began walking back toward the main gate. He was now moving parallel to their position. The unexpectedness of the move bought him precious seconds as the killers were forced to adjust their approach, momentarily confused by his change in direction.

From the corner of his eye, he saw them increase their pace. One circled wider, attempting to flank him from the left. Another moved directly to intercept his path to the gate. The third held his distance, ready to close the trap once Mardonius was engaged with the others. They kept it all too loose, this could only mean there must be a fourth somewhere.

Mardonius measured the distance to the gate against the speed of his pursuers. To run would make it clear this was not a game, they would be able to attack with impunity then. He needed an advantage, an opening while they were still keeping up the illusion.

A sideways glance showed Licarin still watched from above, his expression unchanged. Did he feel satisfaction? Or was there emptiness, the knowledge that even this wouldn't bring Daffir back? Mardonius couldn't waste thought on such questions. Survival demanded his complete focus.

The nearest killer was barely twenty paces away now, his mace held low in a deceptively casual grip that would allow for an upward strike to the ribs or throat. His eyes held the flat determination of a man doing a job, nothing personal, which made him all the more dangerous, professionals didn't make mistakes of passion.

Mardonius squared his shoulders, as if preparing to confront the man directly. Let them think him a fool, an old soldier too accustomed to facing threats head-on. Let them underestimate the man who had survived when boys like Daffir had not. Sometimes, survival wasn't about being the strongest or fastest - it was about being the one willing to do whatever was necessary.

The fourth man appeared just as Mardonius had anticipated, a guard positioned at the gate. He was watching the trap close with the patient eyes of a seasoned killer. Unlike the pretend recruits, he made no effort to disguise his purpose, hand resting openly on a long dagger at his hip. The gate guard who had checked Mardonius' papers earlier was nowhere to be seen, replaced, or perhaps paid to look the other way. Four against one, with Licarin watching from above like some dark deity demanding sacrifice.

Mardonius sized up the gate guard with the experienced eye of a veteran who had spent years making life-or-death decisions based on the smallest details. The man was large, heavily muscled, his stance solid but he favoured his right leg ever so slightly. An old injury perhaps, or simply the natural tendency of a right-handed fighter? Either way, it was a weakness, and

Mardonius had survived by exploiting precisely such flaws.

The three behind him were closing fast. Twenty paces back, their footsteps accelerating from walk to run as they realised he was making for the exit. No more time for pretence. Mardonius quickened his own pace, moving toward the gate guard with the confident stride of a man who expected to be let through.

"Stop there, you," the guard called, his hand moving to draw his blade. The informal address "you" confirmed what Mardonius already knew. This man was no Legion guard enforcing barracks protocol; he was one of Licarin's hired killers, using military authority as a convenient mask.

Mardonius didn't slow. Instead, he shifted his weight to his back foot, his hand reaching toward his belt as if fumbling for his token. The guard's eyes followed the movement, it was only a fraction of a second's distraction, but that was enough. Mardonius exploded forward, not into the frontal attack the guard expected, but in a sweeping lateral move.

The sliding kick connected precisely where he'd aimed, the side of the man's right knee where the leg already showed weakness. Mardonius put the full weight of his forward momentum behind it, feeling the sickening give of ligaments tearing beneath his boot. The guard's shout of pain transformed into a strangled gasp as his leg buckled. He pitched forward, dagger half-drawn, suddenly fighting gravity rather than his intended target.

Mardonius was already up and past him, using the man's falling body as a shield against the pursuers. He heard the rush of air as one of the weighted training maces swung where his head had been a moment before. No time to look back, they'd caught up too fast. In an attempt to guard himself from repercussions Licarin had left the main gate unguarded and it beckoned to him like a lighthouse, a rectangular promise of freedom barely fifteen paces away.

A shout from behind: "Stop him!" The voice carried the unmistakable edge of command, not Licarin himself, but certainly someone accustomed to being obeyed. Mardonius pumped his legs harder, feeling the burn of muscles protesting sudden demand. Ten years in the Legion had kept him fit and he was proud that even his month's long travels from the East of Rande to its centre-most city had not made him soft.

Boot steps pounded behind him, gaining. The closest pursuer was quick, his footfalls light and rapid. Mardonius judged the distance by sound alone. He was already too close and still closing fast. Five paces from the gate, he felt rather than saw, the swing of a weapon toward his back. Pure instinct made him veer sharply left, the mace whistling past his ear close enough to stir his hair.

Overcommitted, the attacker's momentum carried him forward, off-balance from the missed strike. Mardonius' hand shot out, grabbing the man's tunic at the shoulder and using his own forward drive propelled him face-first into the stone wall beside the gate. The crack of impact was followed by a groan and the clatter of the dropped weapon.

Mardonius burst through the gate at full sprint, nearly colliding with a startled group of actual recruits entering the barracks. Their confusion created a momentary barrier between him and his hunters, it was a gift he didn't waste.

The streets outside the barracks were crowded with mid-morning traffic; merchants, citizens, soldiers on leave. Mardonius cut sharply right, then immediately left, ducking under a cart laden with vegetables. He weaved through the press of bodies, changing direction with each intersection, using the chaos of the city as a shield.

Behind him, shouts of pursuit gradually became muffled by distance and the general din of Rande at midday. Mardonius didn't slow his pace. Licarin's men wouldn't give up easily, not with their employer watching their failure from that window. They would spread out, check obvious routes, question bystanders.

He darted down an alley barely wide enough for his shoulders, emerged into a small square where children played some complicated game with stones and chalk marks, then plunged into the shadowed interior of a Temple to Eanna in her guise as the Mother of Soldiers. He thought this fitting as the cool darkness enveloped him. Worshippers sang and danced, their devotions creating an audio screen that masked any sounds of pursuit. Mardonius moved reverently along the wall, head bowed as if in worship, until he reached a side door that opened onto yet another winding street.

Each breath scraped his throat raw, leaving a metallic tang in his mouth. Sweat plastered his civilian clothes to his body. His right ankle throbbed where he'd wrenched it during the sliding kick, and his forearm stung from a glancing blow he hadn't even registered during the frantic escape. Small injuries, easily ignored in the moment of crisis, now demanded attention as the immediate danger receded.

Still, he pushed on, following the maze-like streets deeper into the city's poorer quarters. Here, the buildings leaned drunkenly into each other, creating patches of permanent shadow even at midday. The streets narrowed, then widened unpredictably. Twice, he doubled back on his route, checking for pursuers before changing direction again.

Only when he was certain he'd lost them did Mardonius allow himself to slow to a walk. His chest heaved with exertion, each breath a reminder of how close he'd come to having no breaths left at all. The familiar weight of failure settled on his shoulders, not failure to escape, but failure to anticipate Licarin's hatred. He should have known better than to walk openly into the barracks. Should have found another way to claim his payment. Should have...

No.

There was no profit in such thoughts. What mattered now was survival. What few possessions he owned, including his weapons, waited at an inn near the eastern gate, a lifetime away across this sprawling city. And after that? Five gold coins that now seemed as unattainable as the stars. His rightful payment, his future, held hostage by a grief-maddened commander who wouldn't rest until he had blood for blood.

But beneath the despair an awareness blossomed: Licarin had made his move and exposed his intentions, his one chance for ambush was lost.

The sun had reached its zenith, beating down on the city with merciless intensity. Mardonius merged with the flow of humanity filling Rande's streets, just another face in the crowd. A man with a past he could no longer admit and an increasingly uncertain future. With each step that carried him deeper into the city's embrace, the weight of what he'd lost, not just coins, but the dream they represented, threatened to pull him under.

The Sleeping Fox Inn crouched at the junction of three narrow streets, its weathered sign swinging lazily in the afternoon breeze. Mardonius approached from the west, keeping to the shadows, pausing at each corner to scan before proceeding. Three times he'd circled the building, checking rooftops and alleyways for the tell-tale stillness of a waiting ambush. Only when he was certain the area was clear did he approach the inn's side entrance, never the main door, a habit that had saved his life more than once on the northern border.

The common room smelled of stale beer and old smoke, its sparse afternoon clientele clustered around tables worn smooth by countless elbows and spilled drinks. A bored barmaid with hair braided tight against her scalp, her movements mechanical, eyes distant. Mardonius noted each patron automatically: two merchants discussing prices in low voices, an old man dozing in the corner, three labourers sharing a pitcher of what was most likely watered-down ale. No military posture among them, no hands too clean for their clothes, no eyes that tracked his movement with more than passing interest.

The innkeeper looked up from his ledger, recognition flickering across his pale, pudgy face. "Thought you'd be gone by now," he said with feigned interest. "Said you were just leaving your things for the morning."

"Change of plans," Mardonius replied, keeping his tone light despite the knot of tension between his shoulder blades. "Need my pack now. Room still secure?"

"Aye, none been up there but the girl to sweep." The innkeeper gestured toward the narrow staircase with his chin. "Key's still yours till sunset."

Mardonius climbed the stairs, each creaking step a small alarm that would warn him if he was followed. The hallway above stretched long and dim, lit only by a single window at the far end. He unlocked the third door on the right, entered with caution. The room was small and sparse. It had a narrow bed, a three-legged stool, a peg on the wall for clothing. Exactly as he'd left it, his possessions untouched.

His pack leaned against the far wall, the weight of his ring mail making it sag slightly to one side. He checked each item methodically. The healing kit with its bandages and herb pouches. Travel rations, enough for six days if he needed to rely on them. His bedroll, tightly bound with leather straps. All present, all undisturbed.

The metal shield lay where he left it this morning. His mace hung from a hook beside the bed. Finally, the longbow, his most prized possession. Wrapped in oiled cloth and sealed against moisture, the ash wood remained as resilient as the day it was gifted to him.

Mardonius packed everything like he had done a thousand times before, each item finding its designated place. The mace at his belt, the shield across his back, the bow case secured to the side of his pack. He changed into his leather armour, the familiar weight settling on his shoulders like an old friend's embrace. Strange, how much more himself he felt when fully armed, despite his efforts to appear civilian these past months.

Downstairs, he gave the last of his copper coins to the innkeeper, the cost of last few day's stay and food. The innkeeper swept the coins into a pouch with a nod but no comment then turned back to his books. Just seven bronze bits left, enough for a common room's meal and a tankard of ale.

What to do now?

He turned to leave, calculating his next move. He needed to get out of Rande - immediately - but the gates would be watched. Licarin's reach might not extend to every guard in the city, but Mardonius couldn't risk finding out which ones were in the commander's pocket.

"Archer, aren't you?"

The voice came from his left, rough and low. A man sat alone at a corner table, nursing a full tankard of something dark. He was not there when Mardonius had come in off the street. His leather armour bore the scuffs and stains of hard travel, and a sword hung at his hip, not military issue, but well-maintained. A mercenary's blade.

Mardonius assessed the man before responding. Broad shoulders, sun-darkened skin, a scar that disappeared into his beard. The calluses on his visible hand spoke of years gripping a weapon. Not one of Licarin's men then; his posture was all wrong, too relaxed, too open.

"What makes you say that?" Mardonius asked, neither confirming nor denying.

The man gestured toward the wrapped bow with his tankard. "That ain't no fishing pole on your back, is it? And you don't look rich enough to own a longbow for sport, do ya. Military issue, unless I miss my guess." He pushed out the chair opposite him with one foot. "Sit. Might have something of interest to you."

Mardonius hesitated. Every instinct screamed to keep moving. To put as much distance between himself and this city as possible. But the man's next words gave him pause.

"Need a guard for a four-day job. Caravan leaving the north gate in a few hours. Pays a copper up on completion with all meals provided."

Four days. The north gate was away from the barracks, away from Licarin. A copper coin would buy food enough to tide him over until he found more work. More importantly, caravans travelled with their own guards, their own protection. Safety in numbers, at least temporarily.

"What's the cargo?" Mardonius asked, finally taking the offered seat.

"Textiles, mostly. Some spices. Nothing worth dying for." The mercenary took a slow sip from his tankard. "But the road's been seeing more bandits lately. Employer wants extra security."

"Bandits I can handle." Mardonius kept his face impassive. What he didn't say was that compared to Licarin's vendetta, bandits were a welcome change of threat.

"Thought you might." The mercenary extended a hand. "Caravan leaves from Dender's Warehouse. Show up ready to ride by sixth bell."

"I'll be there." Mardonius clasped the offered hand briefly, then rose. No need for names, no need for histories. In the mercenary profession, the less known, the better.

Outside, the afternoon had begun its slow slide toward evening. Mardonius adjusted his pack straps, feeling the weight of his possessions. All he had left in the world settled against his back. A copper coin for four days' travel. As a plan it was barely more than no plan at all, but it was movement away from the noose that had nearly closed around his neck this morning and there would be anonymity in the group. Gate guards generally checked the goods only, they rarely bothered with who was guarding them. He chuckled to himself when he realised he did not even ask where the caravan was headed.

He set off toward the northern quarter, keeping to back streets with senses alert for any sign of pursuit. Somewhere above the city's tangled streets, Licarin would be issuing new orders to his men, spreading the net wider. But for now, Mardonius had found a small tear in that net, just large enough to slip through, if he moved quickly enough.

The caravan would be his lifeline out of the Royal City. After that? One problem at a time. He'd survived a decade of war by focusing on the immediate threat, the next hill to take, the next enemy to face. Today was no different. Survive. Escape. Regroup. And perhaps, one day, claim what was rightfully his; if not the gold, then at least a future free from looking over his shoulder.

CHAPTER 1

14ᵗʰ Day of Spring.

Three sharp knocks, a pause, then two more in quick succession. Mardonius bolts upright, instantly alert. The pattern is seared into his mind. Three knocks: Wagon Master requested. Two knocks: Not urgent. A call for an officer and specific to his former rank. Someone outside knows him, or at least who he used to be.

He sits up instantly, hand already reaching for the mace beside his bedroll. The movement is fluid, betraying none of the stiffness a civilian might show after sleeping on a bedroll laid out on a hard wooden floor. His eyes adjust quickly to the gloom.

The cloth storehouse smells of camphor wood and dye, overlaid with the sharper notes of dried herbs. Bundles of lavender and rosemary hang from the low rafters. Their fragrance is pleasant enough, but their true value is practical, keeping the valuable textiles stored in this room safe from pests. Wooden shelves line the walls, each laden with bolts of fabric. Linen, cotton, wool, there are even a few rolls of silk. All arranged by type, colour, and quality. Master Gynn's Exotic Goods is clearly prosperous and well-organised. Nothing is out of place, except perhaps the guest who slept among the merchandise.

"Enter." Mardonius says, voice steady. He eyes his mace to ensure it is within reach.

The hide covering the entrance is pushed aside, revealing a young man in a simple tunic. A warehouse worker, barely old enough to grow a proper beard.

Mardonius grunts an acknowledgment as he studies the boy. "Who taught you that knock?"

The boy's expression flickers with momentary confusion. "One of the guards, sir. Said it'll wake you up sharp. It is almost time to leave."

"Thank you." he says, hiding his concerns behind a veneer of calm. The lad leaves. Alone again, Mardonius' jaw clenches.

Sharp indeed. He'd been careful on the journey from Rande, offering no personal details beyond his name, keeping his military bearing disguised beneath a civilian slouch. Yet somehow, they know. Not just that he served, many men did, but his precise rank.

Moonlight washes the wall in indigo. Outside the cloth storehouse, horses snort, boots scrape on wooden boards, voices murmur. Four days' journey at a merchant's pace had been too slow for a soldier's blood, but it was safe and anonymous enough he'd thought, until now.

The knock is a military tradition, used only among soldiers. Someone here must be ex-Army, intimate with its protocols. Mardonius feels that familiar knot of unease: he's exposed. If they know his rank, what else have they guessed? His fugitive status? Licarin's reward on his head?

He pulls on his boots, his mind racing with thoughts. The high pay that attracted him now seems less about hazardous cargo or a potential trap and more about valuing his expertise. It couldn't be Licarin, he wouldn't need subtle tactics this far from the city, a knife in the ribs would be enough.

He decides his best ally remains silence.

Mardonius calmed himself with the morning ritual that the Legion established as the cornerstone of each day when action was to be expected.

He runs his hand along the beautiful unstrung longbow which is protected from the elements within its oiled leather carrying case. It is his pride and joy and a gift from his unit upon the conclusion of his ten years. He unwraps its bowstrings, allowing his fingers to trace the three lengths of oiled cord. The primary string shows a slight fray at one loop, the two backups are flawless. He seals them back in their pouch against the damp night air.

Ten arrows lie on his bedroll. He checks each shaft for straightness, each fletching for security. Eight bear the standard military point. Two carry heavy, barbed heads for big game, or desperate foes. He arranges them in the quiver: lethal precision at the bottom, general heads ready on top.

His mace usually hangs from its hook on his belt. It too is a gift, this time from his then commander as a sign of his ascension to the Rank of Tent Master: commander of 8. The weapon sits in his hand with the familiarity of a lover, its weight and balance extensions of his own arm.

He runs his thumb along the shaft, checking for splits or weaknesses in the wood. Finding none, he examines the metal head, the flanges still protruding enough to puncture armour at the right angle. It bears a dent on one side, a memento from deflecting a Twisted's bone club three summers ago. He quickly polishes the metal with a corner of his cloak.

The shield requires more thorough inspection. He unwraps it from its protective covering, examining the metal facing for any signs of rust or weakness. The blue star marking his unit in the Eastern Legion remains bright beneath the leather cover he'd stitched himself. The star was his insignia of command, and a marker of the First Wagon, a symbol that once filled him with pride but now a dangerous identifier. He tests the shield's rim for any give, any hint that the wood beneath the metal facing might be compromised. A shield that fails in combat means death, and Mardonius has no intention of dying because of poor maintenance.

His leather armour is supple from regular treatment with oil. He shakes it out, checking each seam and strap for signs of wear. It's much lighter than the ring mail bundled in his pack, offering less protection but greater mobility and silence. The trade-off is calculated. Ring mail announces a warrior of means, draws attention he can't afford. Better to appear a common sell-sword in serviceable leather than a professional in military-grade protection.

He dons the armour instinctively, fingers finding buckles without needing his eyes to guide them. Each strap is tightened to the same tension, allowing free movement without gaps in coverage. The leather sits against his body like a second skin, worn to conform to his muscles and movements after years of use.

Last, his coin pouch. The leather bag hangs flat and light against his hip, containing just the copper they paid him last night added to his seven brass bits. Not even a silver to his name. The pouch is waterproof, double-stitched at the seams, a quality container embarrassed by its meagre contents. After a decade of service. After earning the highest rank possible for a non-noble. After leading men into battle and bringing most of them home again, his worth has been reduced to eight small discs of the most common metal. He ties the pouch closed, the familiar knot tight and secure. A copper and seven won't buy much beyond a single meal and a night's lodging in the poorest inn.

He has been promised two silver for this next job though, but it's still a far cry from the five gold coins the Army owes him. Five gold coins that might as well be on the moon for all his ability to claim them.

His fingers brush against the fabric of his tunic, stiff with the dust of travel. The journey from Rande has left its mark on his clothes and boots alike. Four days northward along The Mountain Way, moving through an ever-changing landscape. The first day had taken them through the cultivated fields and orderly orchards surrounding the capital. The farms gave way to the vast undulating grassy plains that form Rande's heartland, seas of green stretching to the horizon, broken only by the occasional copse of trees marking a spring or stream.

By the third day, the terrain had begun to rise with gentle hills swelling from the plain like the shoulders of sleeping giants. And always ahead, growing larger with each day's travel, the breath-taking wall of the Worldspine Mountains, their snow-capped peaks piercing the sky like the spears of titans.

The dust clings to his boots and the hem of his cloak still. The fine red-brown particles that rise from The

Mountain Way with each traveller's footstep. It's different from the yellow dust of the eastern borderlands where he'd spent most of his service. Different, too, from the sandy soil near the south eastern coast. This dust speaks of the northern reaches, of proximity to the mountains and their particular mix of lesser earth and ancient hard stone.

Now he's in Aissentur, a town of perhaps a thousand souls nestled where the plains prepare for their serious climb toward the mountains.

The caravan had arrived as evening shadows stretched across the streets, the last light of day gleaming on the walls of the keep high on the hill that dominates the eastern edge of town. A frontier settlement, though 'frontier' suggests something raw and unfinished. Aissentur is neither. It's established, sturdy, a place built to endure in the shadow of both mountains and the ever-present threat of the Brotherhood of Tszzarb just twenty miles to the north.

The town had offered food and shelter. Both were welcome after days on the road.

He finishes with stretches drilled into him on day one of Legion training, loosening muscles that must not be allowed to betray him. Pack and weapons gathered, he's ready to meet the driver and face whatever lies beyond.

Master Gynn's operation had impressed him immediately. It appeared organised and prosperous without being ostentatious. A merchant who values precision and reliability, qualities Mardonius respects. On top of that the merchant's people had given him free lodgings for the night and offered more work. Two silver coins, no less, for just two days' work. Given his options, it's a bargain.

Pushing aside the leather patch which covered his room's entrance Mardonius enters a space rich with the mingled scents of commerce. Wood, leather, lamp oil, and beneath it all, the particular smell of wealth. It is not the gaudy perfumes of nobility though but the earthy aroma of goods moving from one place to another, of profit carefully cultivated and harvested.

The space is large enough for 2 wagons to sit side-by-side, though only one is here now. Narrow barred windows are set high in the wooden walls but the only light is provided by oil lamps hanging from hooks at regular intervals. Their flames dance in the drafts created by moving bodies, casting long, fluid shadows across the flagstone floor.

At the centre of this hive stands a single wagon, its wooden bed already half-filled with goods. Six workers circle it in a choreographed dance of loading and securing, each movement efficient, each placement deliberate. They remind Mardonius of a well-drilled unit preparing for march.

"The seed is to go beneath the canvas cover," directs a hawk-faced man with ink-stained fingers. "The grain sacks must be balanced against the left wall of the wagon bed." The scribe holds a scroll of parchment, consulting it between directives, making small marks with a quill. His eyes miss nothing, darting from the wagon to his list and back with hummingbird quickness.

Mardonius watches from near the doorway, assessing both the operation and his role within it. The wagon itself is solidly built, its wheels recently greased judging by the sheen visible even from this distance. The body is constructed of seasoned oak, the joints reinforced with metal bands. A merchant's wagon, not military issue, but built to similar standards of durability.

The cargo itself tells a more complex story. Bolts of common fabric. Barrels strapped securely against the front board. Multiple sacks of foodstuff. Crates of varying sizes, some bearing the distinctive red seal of the harbour masters of Tearsport well over a tenday's march to the southwest. An interesting mix of goods but nothing that appears to be worth a silver to guard. Either Master Gynn greatly overvalues security or there is a specific threat on the route. Of course there is the matter of the missing courier, but that is another silver's worth apparently...

Workers move with practiced skill.

A young loader stumbles slightly, nearly dropping a small crate. The scribe's reprimand is immediate but controlled; stern words delivered at precisely the volume needed to reach the offender without disrupting the entire operation. The worker reddens, secures his load, and continues with heightened attention.

This is no amateur operation. The loading follows a pattern Mardonius recognises from his days organising supply wagons in the Legion. Heavy items low and centred for stability. Valuable goods positioned for easy defence. Weight distributed to prevent strain on any single wheel or axle. Master Gynn clearly employs people who understand the logistical realities of moving goods through potentially hostile territory.

"So you're the one who'll be my shield today?" a voice says from behind him.

Mardonius turns, careful not to show surprise at how closely the man had approached without his notice. The speaker is older than Mardonius' 27 years. His face weathered by sun and wind, with the particular squint around the eyes that comes from years of peering into distances. His clothing is simple; a stained tunic, leather pants and worn sandals. The quilted armour he wears over it all shows signs of poor maintenance.

"Lukkar," the man introduces himself with a nod rather than an extended hand. "I drive the wagon. You watch my back."

Mardonius turns back to watch the loaders, "I guard where I'm told to guard," he replies simply.

"Good," Lukkar says, "We leave before dawn. Straight run to Swansbane, a night there, immediate return."

"Understood." Mardonius says. The name Swansbane doesn't register at all but curiosity is a luxury for men with fuller coin pouches.

The warehouse continues its productive hum around them, the wagon gradually filling with its carefully arranged cargo. Soon they'll be on the road and whatever secrets Master Gynn's operation holds will have a chance to reveal themselves. No matter what, Mardonius will be vigilant.

Suspiciously generous pay rarely comes without suspiciously demanding work.

The courtyard stretches before him like a canvas painted only in abrupt splashes of moonlight or shadow. A stone well dominates the centre of the yard, its circular wall rising to waist height, capped with a wooden roof supported by four posts. The winch mechanism gleams with regular oiling, another sign of attention to detail.

Mardonius crosses to the well, aiming to fill the empty waterskin which he normally hangs from his back rack. The rope feels rough against his palms as he works the winch, hears the gentle splash of the bucket not too far below. The water that fills his drinking skin is cold enough to ache against his fingers, drawn from aquafers that lead to the local lake. He takes a testing sip before filling the skin completely. The taste is sharp with minerals, carrying the distinct tang of water that's filtered through mountain stone. Clean and bracing, it shocks his system fully awake in a way that even his disciplined morning routine couldn't achieve.

As he secures the cap on his waterskin, movement near the building catches his attention. Guards stand beside the heavy wooden doors that close off Master Gynn's Warehouse from the streets of Aissentur. Two men, casually resting their weight on the spears; quiet and observant.

Mardonius meets their eyes across the courtyard. One guard's posture shifts subtly, becoming rigidly formal. His left hand strikes his chest in the distinctive salute of the Army, knuckles against heart, a gesture of respect from one soldier to another. Without thought, Mardonius' body betrays him. His own fist rises to mirror the salute, muscle memory overriding conscious decision. The moment he completes the gesture regret floods through him. Such instinctive responses are precisely what he's been trying to suppress, the military bearing he's been desperate to disguise since fleeing the Royal City of Rande.

The guard's mouth curves in a knowing half-smile. The look says more clearly than words: I see you, soldier. I know what you are. The quiet acknowledgment of shared experience.

Mardonius lowers his hand, still cursing inwardly at his lapse. Four days of careful self-presentation are being undone in a single morning. But the damage runs deeper than this moment. The guard's immediate recognition means Mardonius' efforts at disguising his background were less successful than he'd hoped. How much do they know? His rank as Wagon Master, clearly, from this morning's knock. Do they know of Licarin's vendetta?

Master Gynn's operation presents the face of a successful merchant enterprise and perhaps that's truly what it is. But it's staffed by men with military training, men who recognise the signs in others because they carry it within themselves. But the specific knowledge of his rank suggests something more targeted. Either Master Gynn makes a habit of learning detailed backgrounds on all potential hires, or Mardonius himself was of particular interest. Neither possibility sits comfortably with a man trying to disappear.

The staffroom is entered from the warehouse. The room is spacious but not wastefully so, every inch devoted to the essential business of feeding a working household. Clean swept stone floors, blackened walls above the main hearth from years of cooking fires. Three small tables with benches occupy the space closest the room's uncovered entry way.

Scents layer the air in complex strata. Closest to the door, the sharp tang of vinegar where someone has recently scrubbed a table clean. Deeper in it is the rich aroma of meat and herbs simmering in the black iron pot suspended over the main hearth; a hearty stew that speaks of both prosperity and practicality. Not the thin gruel of a miserly operation nor the extravagant waste of a noble's kitchen, but substantial fare meant to fuel a day's honest work.

Mardonius moves toward the hearth, noting how a guard, apparently off duty, acknowledges him but doesn't pause in kneading a sore calf muscle. Near the fire, a stack of thick crusted camp bread sits beside a ladle worn smooth from years of use. No servant appears to serve him, nor does he expect one. In establishments like this, men feed themselves unless rank dictates otherwise.

He takes a bread roll from the stack, cracks it open to create a hollow. The ladle dips into the pot with a soft splash bringing up chunks of meat swimming in thick brown gravy specked with herbs. Steam rises from the stew carrying the scents of onion, bay, and something earthy that might be mushrooms or root vegetables. He pours the ladle-full into his bread bowl.

The initial bite tingles on his tongue, serving as a gentle reminder to be patient. He blows on the meal, observing the rich gravy rippling. The second bite is just right; hot enough, with the meat tenderly giving way to his teeth.

This simple dish becomes exceptional through careful attention. The meat is cooked until perfectly tender, herbs are added at the ideal moment to maintain their flavour, the salt is balanced thus enhancing but not overpowering the dish. It's truly satisfying.

Mardonius stands by the hearth while eating, his back against the wall, allowing him a clear view of the door. He can't remember a time when he ate without first evaluating exits and potential threats. Even as a child in his uncle's humble home, he preferred seats facing the door. It is a habit that began long before his military service and proved beneficial throughout it.

The warmth of the fire seeps through his clothing, chasing away the last of the morning chill. Outside these walls, Aissentur shivers in the grip of early spring, frost still claiming the shadows where moonlight can't reach. This far north, with the Worldspine Mountains looming over the landscape, winter relinquishes its hold reluctantly, retreating inch by grudging inch as the days lengthen. The kitchen's heat is a luxury Mardonius appreciates with the full awareness of a man who has spent too many nights huddled beneath thin blankets in threadbare army tents. Or worse, beneath no roof at all with only his cloak between his body and the indifferent stars.

His thoughts turn to the traveller rations secured in his pack, grains, nuts and dried fruits, compact and long-lasting, chosen for their combination of energy and portability. Nearly a week's worth, carefully wrapped to protect against moisture and pests. Some might call it paranoia to maintain such supplies when employed by a clearly prosperous merchant, but Mardonius knows better. The world doesn't distinguish between the prepared and unprepared until the moment preparation becomes survival.

He is not even sure if this contract will provide meals along the road. The job did not specify it and Mardonius hadn't asked, unwilling to appear concerned with such details. Some employers consider food an expected provision for hired guards. Others expect men to fend for themselves from their payment. With the promised coin not forthcoming until the job's completion, Mardonius won't be purchasing supplies along the way unless absolutely necessary. If needs be, he will hunt.

The stew in his trencher diminishes steadily as he eats with the opportunistic hunger of a soldier conditioned to take sustenance when available regardless of appetite or circumstance.

Master Gynn's operation continues to impress with its attention to detail and quality. The staff room, like the warehouse, functions with quiet capability. The stew itself represents the same philosophy, substantial without being extravagant, carefully prepared but not fussy. The kind of meal that acknowledges the dignity of labour without pretension. A meal that assumes its recipients deserve proper nourishment, not merely sustenance. An employer like Gynn must be well-loved by his people. Such treatment of employees suggests unusual generosity and excellent leadership.

He swallows the last gravy-soaked crust of bread. The meal sits warm in his stomach, a pleasant weight that grounds him in the present moment. He chuckles to himself: an army fights on its stomach.

Before stepping through the heavy wooden door that lead back to the courtyard, Mardonius dons his grey hooded cloak. The wool is thick enough to block the northern wind, it was one of the first things he sourced for himself once he left the Legion. He bought it in early autumn to help prepare for the meandering march he made to the Capital. Like the leather wrap covering his shield, the cloak serves a dual purpose, protection from the elements and concealment of what lies beneath. He drapes it over his shoulders, adjusting the fall to ensure his leather armour is well-hidden. The final effect is intentionally nondescript, a traveller of no particular distinction or origin.

Pulling the door open, the northern spring again assaults him with brutally cold air. The chill is immediate and merciless, cutting through his layers of clothing as though they were gossamer. This far north, with the Worldspine Mountains looming in the distance, spring is more calendar notation than reality. The darkness still bites with winter's teeth even as the lengthening days promise eventual relief.

His breath plumes white in the darkness, a visible betrayal of life in a world temporarily suspended between night and morning. The courtyard stones radiate cold through the soles of his boots in sharp contrast to the kitchen's warmth. Stars and moon wheel overhead, crystal clear in the mountain air, their light providing just enough illumination to navigate by as his eyes again adjust to the darkness.

The streets of Aissentur lie mostly quiet around him, its inhabitants still huddled beneath blankets or clustered around hearth fires. Bakers would be feeding bread into their ovens for the morning rush. From somewhere claps the rhythmic sound of a wood being chopped.

Mardonius stands motionless, letting his senses absorb what his eyes cannot see clearly. The smell of wood smoke hangs in the still air from a hundred chimneys exhaling the scent of pine and oak. Beneath it, the ever-present smell of night soil and animal dung that permeates any settlement built around travel and trade.

To the east, the faintest suggestion of grey lightens the horizon, it may not be dawn yet but this is the first indication of the sun's eventual arrival. In another hour that grey will warm to pink, then orange, then the full brightness of day. But now, in this liminal space between night and morning, the world still belongs to those comfortable with shadow.

CHAPTER 2

The Wedded Road, named for its path parallel to The Mountain Way, stretches out before the warehouse like a grey scar between homes, its packed earth and scattered gravel dull in the dim pre-dawn light. Mardonius stands by the waiting wagon, maintaining a straight posture despite the chill numbing his fingers on his belt. The wagon softly creaks as Lukkar shifts on the driver's seat. It is low on its axles due to being burdened with a fair load of cargo, but from what he can see there appears to be nothing it carries that is worth a fight. Yet the payment suggests otherwise.

"Cold morning," Lukkar mutters, his breath forming vapour that fades into the grey air. "Good for traveling, though." His quilted armour hangs loosely, like he'd never been taught how to secure it properly.

Near the main doors, the warehouse scribe clutches a rolled parchment tightly to his chest like a newborn. He shivers despite the heavy wool cloak draped over his shoulders. Fingers tap against the scroll, each tap oddly loud as the village slowly awakens. He keeps glancing towards the east, where the faintest hint of light suggests the promise of dawn.

A woman stands quietly nearby, watching the proceedings. She's as tall as Mardonius but leaner. Behind her is a donkey.

With little else to occupy him, he observes her. She wears handcrafted leather armour adorned with geometric patterns. Her mid-length hair is braided in the style of the old Do'Ran people who settled this land over 300 years ago. Takaz'Ran, he decides. Clinging to the old ways. Just another minor trader, Mardonius concludes, drawn to the warehouse by the first light. Someone looking to trade tribal goods for more civilised wares, he thinks, dismissing her and turning back to the wagon and the road ahead.

"We're burning daylight," Lukkar grumbles, though the sky is still dark. "The longer we stand here, the later we'll arrive."

"Alright then," the scribe says, finally stepping forward, his voice almost too loud in the stillness before dawn. "Let's finalise this contract so you can be on your way."

The scribe unfurls his parchment with the elaborate ceremony of someone who believes in the mystical power of paperwork. His fingers, stained with the permanent shadows of his profession, smooth curling edges with almost ritual reverence.

"Let all present bear witness," he intones, adopting the formal rhythm witnessing requires. "This contract is between Master Gynn, merchant of goods in Aissentur, and the hired parties named hereafter."

A man and a woman wrapped in thick woollen cloaks shuffle past, casting one bored glance at the gathering before heading towards the town centre. Their indifference highlights how routine Master Gynn's affairs must be. Publicly witnessed agreements are standard fare even in a frontier settlement bristling with traders and guards.

He scans the parchment. "The first assignment involves the safe delivery of goods to the settlement of Swansbane. One wagon and sundry items must be delivered as specified in the manifest. Any goods received as payment must be returned within two days. Payment is one silver coin on successful return."

He pauses, looking at Mardonius. "Mardonius, newly acquainted with Master Gynn, do you accept this task?"

"I do," Mardonius replies, wincing inwardly at how casually his name is spoken in public.

The scribe shifts his gaze back to the parchment. "The second assignment concerns the recovery of a brass scroll case, roughly the length of a man's palm, sealed with wax. A courier left Swansbane two days ago bound for Aissentur and has not arrived."

Mardonius adjusts his stance to give himself a moment for reflection. A missing courier could mean bandits, wild animals, accident or desertion. The offer of another silver coin suggests the case holds something valuable or dangerous.

"The brass case safeguards documents vital to Master Gynn's business. They must remain intact. Payment for this second assignment is one silver coin upon return of the sealed case to Master Gynn or his representative in Aissentur."

Two silver coins total. Enough to cover food and a roof over his head for weeks, maybe a month if he budgets carefully. Enough to buy some breathing room and distance from Licarin's reach. But the thought of the missing courier nags at him. He has learned that lost messengers rarely suffer simple misfortune.

"Any questions before we formalise your acceptance?" the scribe asks.

"I presume no special equipment will be provided for the recovery," Mardonius asks evenly.

The scribe shakes his head. "Master Gynn supplies only the contract and the payment. You choose your own methods."

"I agree to the terms," Mardonius announces.

The scribe makes a small mark beside Mardonius' name with his quill, the scratch of ink echoing in the chilled morning air. Distant birdsong heralds the coming sunrise to a town already stirring.

By the time the reading ends, the eastern sky has brightened to pale grey and the stars have faded. The draft horse stamps its hoof, breath misting. Lukkar remains motionless on the driver's bench, his face unreadable but his posture showing impatience. He is ready to move.

Mardonius checks his gear. Bow, mace and shield are all in place. Ten arrows will have to do. He climbs uneasily onto the wagon alongside the driver.

To Mardonius' surprise the scribe then turned to the Takaz'Ran woman, "Akantha al'Eanna. The same terms apply to you," he said, speaking slower and raising his voice slightly as though bridging a language gap. "Shall I read the full contract again, or is a summary sufficient?"

When he'd addressed Mardonius he'd shown polite deference; now he looked uncertain, unsure of the correct protocol for a tribal warrior. The woman's face gave nothing away.

"Read again," she replied in crisp consonants far sharper than any Randeri accent.

He repeated the entire agreement word for word. Mardonius listened with half an ear, his attention fixed on this unexpected companion as dawn light revealed details lost to the earlier gloom.

Her leather armour was clearly bespoke. It was thicker than standard Royal Army issue and treated with a substance that gave it a subtle sheen. Across the chest and shoulders it bore geometric stitching, they looked like tribal symbols, perhaps marks of rank or protective sigils.

Her spear drew his eye next. The dark wooden shaft was polished smooth by wear and wrapped in leather strips at intervals for grip. Its metal head glowed with recent sharpening, edges honed to lethal precision. A small tassel of leather beads dangled below the spearhead which matched those woven into her braids.

At her belt hung a knife with a scrimshawed bone handle, its blade sheathed in tribal-patterned leather though the steel looked Randeri. He guessed it was a traded blade refashioned to her taste.

Her wooden buckler, strapped to her left arm, offered little more than basic defence compared to his metal-banded shield. What it lacked in coverage it compensated for in manoeuvrability and being strapped in place meant her left hand was essentially free. It was an interesting choice and suggested her fighting style relied on agility rather than strength. Stylised mountains, flames and a bird in flight were carved into its surface, more clan markers or personal totems.

He also spotted a sling coiled around her right wrist. Though simple, a sling after all is just a leather pouch attached to two cords, it was deadly in skilled hands. Even the heavily armoured rightly feared an accurate slinger. One of the leather pouches at her hip probably held ammunition chosen for weight and balance, generally river stones or poured metal shot.

While the scribe delivered the final clauses, Mardonius studied her stance. Feet evenly spaced, knees slightly bent, ready to spring in any direction. A fighter's posture, though relaxed enough to fool the untrained eye.

He'd met traders and cavalry from various Takaz'Ran clans during his service in the Eastern Legion but never engaged so closely with one. They'd kept to themselves and the army never forced the issue.

"The payment terms remain as stated," the scribe concluded. "One silver coin for delivery to Swansbane and back, one for recovery of the brass case. Do you accept?"

Her only sign of hesitation was a firmer hold on the bridle. "I agree," she said, clipped and final. No bargaining, no questions. He decided she'd made her choice long before today.

The scribe marked the parchment beside what must have been her name. Mardonius wondered what she was called among her own people, knowing tribespeople often had names for themselves and names to use with outsiders.

With the formalities concluded, he offers a slight bow and an introduction. The customary greeting among strangers and comrades-in-arms. It is a neutral, professional acknowledgement he has used countless times before.

She ignores him. She pointedly stares straight past him as though he is part of the warehouse wall. The snub feels very intentional.

Mardonius blinked. He'd met distrustful civilians before but never anything this personal, this directed. It was not as though her name was unknown to him, the scribe had announced it, Akantha, openly

Eyes fully adjusted to the gloom revealed more. Her skin is still soft with youth yet already toughened by sun and wind. She has brown eyes the colour of a warhorse's coat and hair pulled into intricate braids threaded with wooden beads and metal clips that click softly as she moves. Her expression remains unreadable.

He hadn't counted on a partner for this job. Partners meant extra worry and could even be a liability if their skills failed to compliment his own. Yet they also brought another pair of eyes, another weapon and someone else to keep watch at camp.

This woman, though. Her gear, her stance, her refusal to engage. All of it said she wanted no part in cooperation which boded poorly for any effective partnership.

With a final sharp tap on the parchment, the scribe seals their fates to Master Gynn's contract. The sound is unnaturally crisp in the morning air, like the snap of a dry twig underfoot during a silent patrol. Mardonius feels the weight of obligation settle across his shoulders, heavier than his shield yet far less protective. The parchment rolls closed with a whisper of finality.

"It is agreed then," the scribe announces, his voice carrying the formal weight of completed business. He tucks the scroll into a leather tube hanging at his belt, patting it once as if to ensure its security. Without another word, he turns and retreats toward the warehouse, his thin silhouette gradually swallowed by the rectangular light of the open doorway. The heavy wooden door swings shut behind him with a solid thud that resonates through the still morning air.

Lukkar shifts his position on the driver's bench. "Bloody scribe... we better not be late to the road," Lukkar says suddenly, breaking the silence. The comment seems directed exclusively at Mardonius, as if the Takaz'Ran woman weren't standing within earshot. His voice is low, almost conspiratorial.

"Why's that?" Mardonius asks, keeping his tone neutral.

Lukkar's weathered face remains expressionless, but something in his eyes shifts. "They close the gates at sundown. No exceptions, not for anyone." He adjusts his grip on the reins, leather creaking between his fingers. "Not even Master Gynn's people."

The statement hangs in the air, the reason unspoken yet implied. Mardonius considers the warning. Gates that close at sundown aren't unusual for frontier settlements, but the absolute nature of Lukkar's statement suggests something beyond normal precaution. Towns vulnerable to bandit raids often enforce strict curfews, but those same towns usually make exceptions for expected arrivals, especially if they are valuable trade caravans.

What waits outside Swansbane's walls after dark that brooks no exceptions? The question settles uncomfortably in Mardonius' mind, another detail that doesn't quite align with what he's been told. Master Gynn's operation continues to reveal layers of complexity beneath its merchant veneer.

Lukkar flicks the reins lightly against the draft horse's broad back. The wagon creaks into motion, wooden wheels grinding against the packed earth of the street. The sound seems unnaturally loud in the quiet morning, a mechanical intrusion into the natural stillness before full dawn.

Behind them, the donkey brays once, a harsh sound somewhere between complaint and announcement. The noise startles a pair of roosting pigeons from their perch atop the warehouse eaves, sending them fluttering into the lightening sky. The Takaz'Ran woman strokes the beast's muzzle with surprising gentleness, murmuring something in her native tongue. The words are lyrical, almost musical, despite their quick, clipped delivery.

As if this Akantha was not already enough of an enigma Mardonius is surprised to see that she, with unexpected grace, swings herself onto the donkey's bare back, settling into position with the ease of long practice. There is no saddle, just a thin blanket secured with a simple strap. Her spear remains in her right hand, its butt now resting against her calf, the point angled slightly backward to avoid threatening the beast's head. She looks for all the world like she was born on the back of this beast but he is not sure he has even seen something so incongruous, a tribal woman riding a donkey like it was a war horse.

The donkey appears untroubled by her weight, stepping forward with the determined plod of an animal accustomed to long journeys. It follows the wagon at a distance of perhaps five paces, its ears flicking forward and back as it takes in the sounds of the wakening town.

The small procession moves through Aissentur's streets, passing shuttered shops and homes where lamps are just beginning to glow behind windows. A baker watches with bored indifference from his doorway, assessing the morning with flour-covered hands propped on his hips, clearly familiar with Master Gynn's wagons and their regular departures.

CHAPTER 3

The wagon lurches forward, its wooden wheels grinding against the packed earth of Wedded Road. Mardonius steadies himself on the bench beside Lukkar, his body adjusting automatically to the vehicle's rhythm. He knows they will have nothing to worry about within the town but he keeps his fingers warm and supple anyway in spite of the cold morning air. Behind them, he hears the steady plod of the donkey's hooves as it carries its prideful rider through streets that haven't fully awakened.

Aissentur unfolds before them in layers of shadow and secondary light. Oil lamps cast pools of amber radiance from scattered windows, their glow too weak to penetrate the lingering darkness fully. Early-rising merchants drag carts into position along the roadside, their movements tainted with sleep yet purposeful with the day's ambition. A woman hangs woollen blankets over a wooden rail, her breath fogging before her face. Two men argue in hushed tones over the placement of a vegetable stand, their voices carrying in the still air despite attempts at quietude.

Mardonius surveys each alleyway as they pass more to keep his mind alert than out of any fear of ambush. He doubts he can afford to stay here too long before Licarin hunts him down, but it doesn't hurt to get a feel for the town anyway.

"Town's getting bigger," Lukkar remarks, breaking the silence. "When I first started driving for Master Gynn, you could throw a stone clear from one end to the other without hitting anything worth mentioning."

Mardonius grunts noncommittally, encouraging conversation without committing to it. Information has value, especially when freely offered.

"The mine's been good to Aissentur," Lukkar continues, seemingly content with Mardonius' minimal response. "Dark Ore brings traders from all over. Regularly see Dwarves even, can you believe it?"

A baker's apprentice emerges from a side street, carrying a tray of fresh loaves. The freshly baked scent wafts toward them, momentarily overpowering the ordinary smells of a waking town: wood smoke, night soil, and the peculiar mineral tang that seems to permeate everything this close to the mountains. Mardonius' stomach tightens in response, reminding him that the stew he ate earlier will need to sustain him until the next meal presents itself.

The wagon wheels transition from packed earth to cobblestones with an increase in noise and vibration. Mardonius glances back, checking on their companion. Akantha sits straight-backed on her donkey, ignoring the occasional curious stare from early risers. Her expression is still a stone wall but her eyes constantly scanning their surroundings with a vigilance that mirrors his own. Despite the humble nature of her mount, she carries herself with the unmistakable dignity of a warrior.

Their route takes them past Bright Lake, its surface a flat sheet of silver in the pre-dawn light. Mist hovers above the water, tendrils reaching toward shore like ghostly fingers. Several small boats are tethered at a modest wooden dock, rocking gently with the water's subtle movement.

"They say eating the fish from the lake grants long life," Lukkar offers, following Mardonius' eyes toward the lake. "But only during the Summer Festival. Any other time, it'll earn you a year in the mines." He chuckles darkly. "Course, nobody survives a year in the mines, so it's really just a death sentence with extra steps."

Mardonius studies the lake with renewed interest. "Strange rule."

"Old tradition. Nobody remembers why." Lukkar says before winking at him, "Some say the Baron just wants to keep the best fishing for himself and his friends."

The road curves gently around the lake's northern edge. As they round the bend, Aissentur Keep comes into view unobstructed by any buildings. It is perched atop the hill that dominates the eastern side of town. Even in the dim light, its silhouette is imposing. It seems to rise organically from the hilltop with solid stone walls punctuated by watchtowers at regular intervals. A single flag hangs limply from the central keep, too distant to identify in the weak light but undoubtedly bearing the Baron's colours.

"Stood firm during the Tszzarbian siege," Lukkar says, tilting his head toward the castle. There's a note of pride in his voice. "Thirty years back now. They thought they'd roll right over us, but the Baron, the old Baron, that is, current one's father, he held them at the walls while the townsfolk took shelter inside."

Mardonius studies the structure with a soldier's eye. It was an excellent defensive position. There were clear lines of sight in all directions and a very difficult approach up a steep hillside. It's stone walls looked thick enough to withstand most siege engines. Yes he decided, it would make a formidable obstacle for an invading force.

"What about the mine?" he asks, recalling mention of a separate fortress.

"Its called Dark Keep. It's north of town. We'll see it but won't pass it today." Lukkar points vaguely northward. "Four miles up The Great Road. That's where they dig the Dark Ore. Prisoners do the digging, guards do the guarding and everyone pretends not to notice when most of the prisoners don't come back up."

They left turn onto Baron's Road, leaving the lake behind. The quality of the buildings changes subtly, the houses are larger and more distinct with better tended gardens and doorways adorned with small decorative touches that speak of modest prosperity. A woman sweeps her doorstep with methodical strokes, pausing only briefly to watch the wagon pass. A craftsman arranges wooden toys on a small table before his workshop, his weathered hands moving with careful precision.

The people here show little interest in the passing wagon.

"Baron's Road leads straight to the keep if you turn right," Lukkar explains. "Named for obvious reasons. Its where those who think they're important live." He chuckles at his own observation. "Merchants, craftsmen who've done well for themselves, retired soldiers who managed to save something. None of the truly wealthy have houses here, they live around the lake, but its comfortable enough."

Mardonius listens while watching a pair of guards patrol the street ahead. Their leather armour bears the Baron's insignia, a mountain peak bisected by a sword. They move with the relaxed confidence of men patrolling familiar territory where trouble is rare but not unheard of. They also ignore the wagon passing.

The sky has lightened considerably during their journey through town, the black of night fading to deep blue, then to the pale grey that precedes dawn proper. The gentlest hint of orange touches the eastern horizon, promising warmth that the current air temperature belies. Mardonius pulls his cloak tighter around his shoulders, the wool scratchy against his neck but effective against the chill.

"We'll hit The Mountain Way soon and travel a couple'a miles out of town," Lukkar says, adjusting his grip on the reins. "From there, it's a straight shot west to Swansbane."

Behind them, Akantha shifts slightly on her donkey, the first movement Mardonius has noticed from her since they departed. He wonders what she makes of this town, so different from the settlements of her people. Does she see the same signs of prosperity and struggle? Or does she view it with the contempt that tribal peoples often reserve for settled communities?

Whatever her thoughts, she keeps them to herself, following in silence as the wagon continues its steady progress through the waking town.

The wagon approaches the intersection where Baron's Road meets The Mountain Way, wheels crunching over a patch of shattered pottery. The corner forms a natural gathering point in Aissentur's layout, as if the town's circulatory system requires this junction to properly distribute its daily commerce. Mardonius notes how the buildings here crowd closer together, creating shadows that the strengthening dawn light hasn't yet penetrated.

"Main crossroads," Lukkar announces unnecessarily, gesturing toward the widening street ahead. "Keep going north up The Mountain Way and it will take you to Tszzarb's Mountain Gate. South gets you back to The Royal City Rande eventually, but you know that." he states with a chuckle as he points out a significant building to their left. "That's where most of the action happens after dark."

The establishment he indicates squats on the corner like a toad that's found a particularly comfortable stone. It is two stories of weathered timber and smoke-darkened stone, with windows shuttered against the morning light despite the sounds of activity within. A wooden sign hangs from an iron bracket above the door, swinging slightly in the morning breeze. The carved image depicts an elf rudely impaled on a spear. Green paint is flaking from the figure's pointed ears, its expression a grotesque mixture of surprise and pain.

"The Stuck Elf," Lukkar says, his tone suggesting the name alone should convey everything Mardonius needs to know. "Best place in town for a drink if you're not too particular about what you're drinking or who you're drinking with."

Mardonius assesses as through it were a tactical exercise. Two entrances visible from their position. The main door facing the crossroads and a smaller one along the side alley. Windows too narrow for easy entry or exit. A defensive layout, whether by design or happenstance.

"Your friend can't go in there," Lukkar adds, jerking his head toward Akantha without actually looking at her. "Takaz'Ran aren't welcome. Owner had some trouble with tribal folk a few years back, lost a few staff for his troubles. Now he's got a strict policy."

The door of the tavern bangs open before Mardonius can respond. A gust of stale air washes over them, carrying the unmistakable bouquet of a establishment dedicated to separating people from their money through the strategic application of alcohol. Sour ale mingles with vomit, sweat, and the peculiar musty scent that develops when too many bodies inhabit too small a space for too many hours. The smell drags Mardonius back to countless frontier outposts where similar establishments offered soldiers brief respite from duty's monotony.

Three men stumble out into the early morning light, their movements unsteady with the remnants of night's indulgence. Their clothing marks them as labourers; coarse woollen tunics stained with the evidence of their trades, leather vests worn smooth at the elbows, boots caked with the mud of yesterday's work. One laughs at something the others have said, the sound too loud in the quiet street, his head thrown back to display a throat mapped with old pockmarks.

The laughter cuts off abruptly when the man's eyes lock onto something behind the wagon. His companions look back, their expressions shifting from confusion to wariness in the span of a heartbeat. The change is subtle but complete. Shoulders tense, hands drop away from belts where knives usually sit, their eyes fix firmly on the ground between their feet.

Mardonius glances back, following the trajectory of their attention. Akantha sits motionless on her donkey, her expression unchanged from the impassive mask she's worn since he first laid eyes on her. She hasn't drawn a weapon or made any threatening gesture, yet these men, each substantially larger than her, have reacted as though confronted by a predator farther up the natural hierarchy than themselves.

Not one of them meets her eyes directly. Instead, they shuffle sideways, giving the wagon a wide berth as they pass, maintaining the maximum possible distance between themselves and the Takaz'Ran woman. They disappear down a side street without another word, their earlier camaraderie temporarily forgotten in their haste to remove themselves from her vicinity.

The response seems disproportionate to the threat. Mardonius has certainly seen similar reactions before, civilians confronted with battle-hardened veterans, ordinary soldiers encountering elite units, but the dynamic here feels different. It is not just simple fear but something more complex. Recognition, perhaps, of consequences they have no desire to provoke.

"They acted like she was carrying plague," Mardonius observes quietly to Lukkar as the wagon passes the tavern.

Lukkar glances around quickly, checking that Akantha remains far enough behind them to avoid overhearing. He leans closer to Mardonius, his voice dropping to just above a whisper.

"Word of advice. Takaz'Ran pride runs deep. They answer disrespect with blood, not words." He straightens up, returning his attention to the road ahead. "Those men know it. Everyone in Aissentur knows it."

The statement hangs between them, heavy with implication. Mardonius considers Lukkar's warning, fitting it against his previous observations of the woman who rides behind them. Her bearing, her weapons, her intentional ignoring of his greeting. All pieces of a puzzle he's yet to fully assemble.

"There was an incident last summer," Lukkar continues after a moment, his voice still low. "Merchant from Rande made some comment about her people. Called them horse-frotters or something equally stupid. She took his eye with a sling stone at thirty paces." He adjusts his grip on the reins. "One of the Baron's men tried to arrest her, wanted to make a name for himself. He instead found three of her tribesmen waiting at the town's common stable. Armed to the teeth they was and looking for an excuse."

"What happened?"

"Baron let her go. Said the merchant got what he deserved for running his mouth. Guard got reassigned out of the area for a season." Lukkar shrugs. "Smart decision. Takaz'Ran live rough and fight rougher. They remember their friends. More importantly, they never forget their enemies."

The wagon turns right onto The Mountain Way, leaving The Stuck Elf and its sour odours behind. A pair of town guards stand at the crossroads, overseeing the morning's transition with bored vigilance. They barely pay attention to Lukkar as the wagon passes but stiffen visibly when they spot Akantha following. Their hands don't move toward weapons, but their posture shifts subtly, weight balanced to enable quick response if needed.

Mardonius studies these reactions with growing interest. He's underestimated his companion, it seems. Not just a tribal girl with handmade weapons but someone known and feared within Aissentur's social hierarchy. Someone with enough reputation to make armed men avoid confrontation on sight.

The realisation shifts his assessment of their partnership. Her refusal to acknowledge him wasn't merely rudeness but a statement of position. She sees no need to establish rapport with him because, in her estimation, she requires neither his approval nor his alliance. They may travel the same road and serve the same employer, but she considers herself neither subordinate nor equal to him.

Mardonius finds himself revising his initial judgment. Where he had seen a young woman with tribal weapons, he now recognises a fighter whose reputation precedes her. If Lukkar tells it true then she is also a warrior for whom respect might be currency more valuable than gold.

The wagon travels north now. The wheels transitioning from cobblestones back to packed earth. The sound changes from sharp clatter to muffled rumble. Mardonius settles himself more comfortably on the bench, considering what he's learned and what it might mean for the journey ahead. Two days to Swansbane and back, plus whatever time the search for the missing courier requires. Not long, but potentially complicated by the cultural currents now apparent.

Behind them, Akantha follows at the same measured distance, her posture unchanged, her expression still unreadable. The donkey plods steadily forward, seemingly untroubled by either the morning chill or the weight of its rider's reputation.

The first true rays of sun break over the eastern horizon. Golden light spills across the landscape, transforming the drab greys of predawn into a spectrum of rich colours. Mardonius squints against the sudden brightness, his eyes adjusting from shadow to illumination. The light doesn't warm him yet, spring mornings in this northern region hold their chill stubbornly, but it promises warmth, a gradual thawing as the day progresses.

The wagon settles into a steady rhythm as wheels find the familiar grooves worn into The Mountain Way by generations of similar vehicles. This road is in better condition than the village streets they've left behind. Its surface is packed hard by regular travel and maintenance. Trade routes receive attention that residential pathways don't merit, their status directly tied to the flow of goods and coin that sustains settlements like Aissentur.

Lukkar relaxes visibly now that they've cleared the town proper, his shoulders dropping, his grip on the reins loosening slightly. "Always feels better once we're on the open road," he remarks, more to himself than to Mardonius. "Town's too crowded these days. Too many eyes."

Mardonius makes a noncommittal sound of agreement, his attention focused on the changing landscape. The transition from urban to rural happens with surprising abruptness. One moment they're passing the last weathered buildings of Aissentur's northern edge, the next they're surrounded by cultivated fields stretching toward distant tree lines.

Young crops push through the dark soil in neat rows, their green shoots barely visible from the road. Workers move through the fields despite the early hour, their backs bent to the eternal labour of coaxing food from earth. A woman straightens as the wagon passes, pressing one hand against her lower back, her face weathered beyond her years by sun and wind and the particular harshness of agricultural life.

"Baron's fields," Lukkar says, noticing the focus of Mardonius' attention. "Most land within sight of the town belongs to him. Leases it to farmers, takes half their yield come harvest." He spits over the side of the wagon. "Good arrangement for the Baron. Less so for them."

The fields give way to pastures where sheep graze in scattered clusters, their white forms stark against the green grass. A boy of perhaps ten summers leans on a crude staff, watching over the flock with a dog at his side. The child raises a hand as the wagon passes, a gesture Lukkar returns with casual familiarity.

"Lain's youngest," he explains. "Good lad. Started watching the northern flock last season."

Mardonius just takes it all in. A hawk circles overhead, its wings barely moving as it rides thermal currents rising from the warming earth. It watches the ground with predatory patience, waiting for some unwary creature to reveal itself. Mardonius feels a kinship with the bird, they share the same vigilance, the same capacity for sudden violence when circumstances demand.

The air smells different here than in town. It is cleaner, carrying notes of soil and growing things rather than the concentrated stew of human habitation. The breeze brings the scent of wildflowers from a meadow to their right, a subtle sweetness that momentarily overpowers the earthier aromas of horse and leather and the lingering human scents that cling to the wagon.

Sounds change too. The constant background noise of town, voices, animals, crafters at work, fades behind them, replaced by the rhythm of hooves, the creak of wagon wheels, the rustle of wind through grass. There are simpler sounds too, less layered but carrying farther across open ground. A dog barks in the distance. A songbird trills from a row of shrubs. The plaintive bleating of sheep drifts across the pasture.

Far to the north, dominating the horizon, the Worldspine Mountains rise in jagged majesty. Even at this distance, their scale impresses, peaks thrust skyward as if trying to pierce the heavens themselves. Snow caps the highest points, gleaming white in the morning sun.

"You can see the Valley of the Black Gate from here on clear days," Lukkar says, pointing toward a seemingly random patch of the mountain range. "Not today, though. Too much haze."

Mardonius follows his gesture, eyes narrowing as he searches for the feature. The Black Gate of Tszzarb is legendary both for its impressive construction and for the forces that poured through it during conflicts with Rande. It sits twenty miles north, according to what he's heard, marking the border between civilised territory and the nature-worshipping dwarf-loving zealots beyond. He'd never been this far north during his service, his duties kept him primarily along the eastern borders where different threats required attention.

"How far to Swansbane?" he asks, returning his focus to the immediate journey.

"Day's travel at wagon pace," Lukkar replies. "We'll easily be there by sunset if we don't stop." He adjusts his position on the bench, shifting weight from one side to the other. "Small settlement. Wouldn't even call it a town. Trading post, really, with a wall around it. Last proper stop before the wilderness to the west."

Mardonius considers this information. A day's journey to deliver the wagon's cargo, another to return with the recovered brass case, assuming they find it quickly of course. Simple enough in theory, though experience has taught him that simplicity rarely survives contact with reality.

Behind them, Akantha stoically follows at her customary distance. The rising sun catches in her hair, highlighting strands of gold among the predominant dark. Her attention seems fixed on the mountains ahead, perhaps finding comfort in their familiar presence. The Takaz'Ran are hills and plains people in the main, if Mardonius recalls correctly. Nomadic horsemen who settled these northern reaches generations ago, maintaining their distinct identity even as they recognised their allegiance to Rande.

The road stretches before them, a pale ribbon cutting through green fields toward the distant mountains. It runs nearly straight here, visible for a mile ahead, every bend and dip exposed to view. No obvious danger presents itself, no sign of the troubles that might have befallen the missing courier. Just the ordinary peace of grasslands fully embracing spring.

Mardonius settles himself more comfortably on the hard bench, adjusting his cloak to let the growing warmth in. His hands drop casually to his lap, but they remain close enough to his weapons for quick access if needed. The road may appear safe, but experience has taught him that appearances rarely tell the complete story. As long as the courier's disappearance remains unexplained a shadow hanging over their otherwise straightforward journey.

Birds dart across the road. Insects hum as the last farmlands fully surrender to the rolling grassy plains.

CHAPTER 4

The Dark Keep rises from the landscape like a tumour of stone, its walls nearly windowless and foreboding in their precision. Mardonius studies it from the wagon bench, his trained eye automatically calculating distances and angles of approach. The massive spoil heap beside the fortress spreads outward in a fan of crushed rock and refuse, grey-black against the green spring grass. Even at this distance, he tastes something metallic on the air, not blood but something equally primal and unsettling.

"Quite the sight, isn't it?" Lukkar says, knowing exactly what Mardonius is looking at. "Most travellers can't stop staring at it, though they always claim they're just admiring the mountains behind."

The keep stands in stark isolation, brutally positioned to dominate the surrounding plains. Unlike the castle in Aissentur's more traditional defences, this structure makes no concessions to aesthetic considerations. Its walls rise straight and severe, unmarked by decorative elements or any signs of comfort. Only the necessary crenulations at the top break the monotony of stone, providing sheltered positions for archers and watchmen.

At the base of the eastern wall, a dark mouth opens towards The Mountain Way. Despite the distance, he can see the movement of small figures, like ants around a disturbed hill. Workers and guards, backs bent to their day's labour, even as the sun's light fails to dispel the feeling of gloom from the dark walls.

The spoil heap tells its own story. Years, decades, of excavation have produced a small mountain of discarded stone, carefully piled to avoid blocking the approach to the keep itself. The material has been worked from ever-deepening digs if the different layers and colorations are anything to go by. Privately he bets that nothing of value would remain in that pile, no doubt it has been sifted and searched with the thoroughness that only profit can inspire.

A breeze carries the scent more strongly toward them. It is a bitter, mineral tang that coats the tongue and makes Mardonius' nostrils flare with instinctive rejection. It is not quite sulphur, but similarly offensive to human senses. It reminds him of the smell of battlefields where magic had been deployed *en-masse*, though less caustic.

"You're wondering about the smell," Lukkar observes, his voice neutral. "That's the Dark Ore. Something about how it reacts with air once it's brought up. The guards say it smells different underground; sweeter, almost. Draws the prisoners deeper, like a siren's call." He makes a hand symbol as if to ward off evil. "Or so they claim. I've never been fool enough to find out myself."

Mardonius accepts the information without comment. The concept of ore with unusual properties isn't new to him. During his service in the Eastern Legion, he'd encountered weapons forged from strange minerals mined from the contested border regions. Blades that held their edge beyond natural limits, arrowheads that could puncture armour that would turn ordinary steel. With the right knowledge and magical skill even simple herbs or gem stones could be enhanced with supernatural effects.

"Baron's soldiers use the keep as their headquarters," Lukkar continues, warming to his topic now that he has an attentive audience. "Upper levels are barracks and armoury. Lower levels belong to the mine and its workers." His mouth twists on that last word, making it clear that "workers" is a euphemism.

"Prisoners," Mardonius says, not a question but a confirmation.

"Aye. Murderers, thieves, rebels, debtors who owe the wrong people." Lukkar's voice lowers slightly, though there's no one close enough to overhear except perhaps Akantha, who maintains her aloof distance. "Sometimes just folk who speak against the Ran, his Barons or refuse to pay what he considers his due. Sentence there's worse than death."

He gestures toward the keep with his chin. "Prisoners work the mines till they drop. No one comes out. Most don't last more than a few months. The air down there eats at their lungs, the Dark Ore blackens their skin until they look more like shadows than men." His voice carries the casual certainty of local gossip, the dark stories everyone accepts as facts without being able to put them to the test.

Mardonius' gaze shifts from the mine entrance to the keep's defences, professional assessment taking precedence over morbid curiosity. He counts eight visible archer positions along the wall facing them, each with clear lines of sight to the approaches. He assumes the he main gate would be a double barrier system with an outer portcullis followed by a killing ground, then an inner gate. Standard design for military installations where defence takes priority over ease of access.

The road they travel passes within half a mile of the keep, close enough for its garrison to intercept any significant traffic but far enough to prevent casual interference with legitimate trade. A strategic calculation, balancing security against commercial necessity. Whoever designed the keep understood both military and economic realities.

What truly impresses Mardonius is the positioning. The keep stands on a slight rise, not dramatic enough to make construction difficult but sufficient to eliminate blind spots in its defensive coverage. To the north, the beginnings of the mountain foothills provide a natural barrier against easy approach from that direction. The spoil heap, intentionally or not, creates an additional obstacle to the south, channelling any potential attackers toward the more heavily defended eastern and western approaches.

"The ore's what makes it all worthwhile," Lukkar says, misinterpreting Mardonius' focused assessment for interest in the mine itself. "Dark Ore takes a higher polish than normal steel, holds an edge longer, doesn't rust. Perfect for weapons, if you've got the skill to work it." His voice carries a note of pride, the natural patriotism of a man discussing his region's claim to fame. "Most important, it is much easier to enchant than any other metal."

"They say the Dwarves taught us how to forge it proper, back when they still came down from the mountains regular-like. Before the war with Tszzarb." He falls silent briefly, his expression suggesting this topic touches on memories he'd rather not disturb.

Mardonius keeps quiet, encouraging him to continue without pressing. The relationship between Rande and the northern kingdom of Tszzarb remains tense even three decades after their last open conflict. Border regions like this would have felt the effects most acutely.

Behind them, Akantha's donkey brays once, the sound startling in the relative quiet. Mardonius glances back. She sits as straight-backed as ever, her posture betraying no discomfort despite hours of riding. Her attention seems fixed on the Dark Keep as well, though her expression remains unreadable. Does she see the same tactical considerations he does? Or is her focus on the darker purpose of the structure: the prisoners below ground, working until death releases them?

He returns his attention to the road ahead, where the mountains rise like titans before them, indifferent to the small cruelties men inflict upon each other in their shadow.

The Worldspine Mountains have grown impossibly large, no longer mere backdrop but a dominant presence. Their jagged peaks catch the morning light, snow fields gleaming white against dark stone that seems to absorb rather than reflect the sun. Mardonius feels their weight in a way maps and military reports can never convey. They are ancient, immovable witnesses to the brief rise and fall of men.

Lukkar rolls his shoulders to fully release muscles warmed by the strengthening sun. His eyes scan the horizon in a relaxed way that acts as counterpoint to Mardonius' constant threat assessment. This is Lukkar's land, he know how to read it.

"See that valley in the mountains?" he asks, pointing toward a distinct depression at the foothills of the otherwise unbroken wall of peaks. "That's where The Mountain Way ends at the Mountain Shield Gate, what we call The Black Gate."

Mardonius narrows his eyes, focusing on the distant feature. At nearly twenty miles' distance the faintest hint of a valley is all he can make out. Apparently this is where a massive stone archway is carved directly into the mountain pass. He saw a drawing of it once. It was flanked by watchtowers that look like natural rock formations until closer inspection reveals them to be constructed. The gate marks more than just a passage through the mountains; it represents the boundary between nations, cultures, beliefs.

"Can't see the details from here," Lukkar continues, "but it's a sight up close. Dwarven work. Two massive doors of iron-banded stone that can close off the entire pass when needed. Haven't been fully shut in decades, not since the peace was settled."

The wagon hits a rut in the road, jostling them both. Lukkar corrects with instinctive ease, barely interrupting his narrative.

"That's where our traders meet theirs now." His hand tightens on the wagon rail, knuckles whitening briefly. "Neutral ground, technically. Our guards stay on our side, their wardens keep to theirs and commerce happily goes on in the shadow of the gate itself."

A flock of birds erupts from a nearby copse of trees, wheeling against the sky before settling again. The horse's ears flick forward, then back, registering the movement without alarm.

"Thirty years back," Lukkar says quietly as if sharing an intimate secret, "they came pouring through that gate. Short swarthy bastards, even the humans, with weapons that cut through armour like butter."

Mardonius studies Lukkar's profile; he notes the tightness around his eyes. He is not merely reciting history but recalling it vividly. The man would have been very young during the Tszzarb War.

"Their magic-users called lightning down from clear skies," Lukkar continues sombrely. "Their crossbow bolts pierced shields and the men behind them with ease. They moved through mountain and hill as if they owned it, terrain that would have slowed any normal army."

The details align with what Mardonius had learned during military training: Tszzarb forces were fewer in number yet superior in equipment and combat skills. Their alliance with the mountain's Dwarves granted access to metallurgy far beyond Randeri capabilities. Their nature priests wielded elemental forces to great and terrible effect.

"They reached Aissentur within a day of crossing that gate," Lukkar states flatly. "We weren't prepared. Peacetime patrols and a minimal garrison meant trouble for us." His voice carried an emptiness reflecting the depth of the painful memories. "The town burned. Families fled to Aissentur Keep and helped our Baron's forces hold their walls.

"They besieged us for sixteen days," he adds grimly as if each word weighs heavy on him still, the rhythm of creaking wood of the wagon accompanying his tale like an echo from those past horrors, "sixteen days of their mages calling storms against our walls and Dwarven sappers trying to undermine our foundations."

Mardonius recognises the confirmation; Lukkar had been there, perhaps as a child among those defending.

"We held." Lukkar's voice sharpens slightly as though reclaiming some lost pride amid sorrowful recollections. "Neither Aissentur Keep nor the Dark Keep fell despite everything they threw at it."

Mardonius can visualise it clearly. A desperate defence against superior forces. Civilians crammed within stone walls meant for far fewer souls. Soldiers fighting fiercely, not for abstract national interests but for home, family and the right to wake up the next morning a free man.

"They might know mountains but they misunderstood the plains. Reinforcements came from the Royal City but it was the cavalry, especially the wild Takaz'Ran riders, that really put the wind up them." Lukkar respectfully nodded to Akantha. "Not enough to drive them back completely, but enough to force a stalemate." A sour look washed across his face as his voice darkened, "Then came the diplomats with their careful words and honeyed concessions."

The bitterness in his tone speaks volumes about his opinions on the peace settlement. Border regions often resent compromises made by distant capitals, viewing wider diplomatic solutions as betrayal of their local sacrifices.

"Terms of the treaty gave them trading rights through the gate, access to our markets under strict regulation. We got guarantees they wouldn't try to attack us again." Lukkar shrugs. "Peace of a sort, though ask anyone in Aissentur and they'll tell you it's just a pause between conflicts."

Mardonius considers this assessment. In his experience, civilians often view military matters in absolute terms.

It was either total victory or shameful defeat with little appreciation for the complex realities that make most conflicts end in compromise. The Eastern Legion had faced similar resentment from border towns who expected complete elimination of threats rather than the managed containment that limited resources made necessary.

"They haven't bothered us since?" he asks, though he already knows the answer.

Lukkar is silent at that before expelling a sigh. His hands flex on the reins, an unconscious gesture. "Lost my older brother on the twelfth day. Lightning strike from one of their spell caster. Nothing left to bury but ash and melted metal. Hard thing to forgive."

The admission hangs between them, requiring no response. Mardonius offers none, respecting the man's grief with silence rather than platitudes. He's heard too many similar stories, delivered in the same flat tone by survivors who've had decades to process their losses but will never quite heal from them.

Behind them, Akantha seems content to follow without joining the conversation. Mardonius glances back at her from time to time. Her expression remains alert but relaxed, her posture easy despite what looks like an uncomfortable riding position on the donkey's bare back. Unlike the men, who remain tensed against memories and potential threats, she appears almost to be enjoying the journey. The open road, the spring air, the freedom of movement after the confines of Aissentur's narrow streets. Her eyes continually scan their surroundings but in the way of a hunter seeking game.

The Takaz'Ran had fought alongside Randerai forces during the Tszzarb War, Mardonius recalls. Their mounted archers had proven particularly effective against the enemy's infantry, harassing flanks and disrupting formations with hit-and-run tactics that complemented the Randerai shield-and-spear defensive style. Perhaps Akantha's relative youth spares her from the personal connection to those events that tightens Lukkar's voice.

Mardonius returns his attention to the road ahead, absorbing what he's learned while remaining alert for any signs of the troubles that might have befallen the missing courier. History provides context, but present dangers demand priority.

The wagon slows as they approach a weathered marker stone marking the junction where a narrower track branches westward from The Mountain Way. Lukkar guides the horse onto this lesser path easily, the wheels grinding against looser soil as they leave the well-maintained thoroughfare behind. The transition feels significant somehow, moving from a road that has existed for centuries onto a track that looks as if it could disappear from a few seasons of neglect.

The terrain changes gradually as they progress. The flat plains soon give way to gentle rolls and swells, like a green sea frozen in mid-wave. Grasses grow taller here, brushing against the wagon's undercarriage with soft whispers. Small copses of trees appear with increasing frequency, their shadows offering brief respite from the strengthening sun.

It's between two such stands of trees that Mardonius spots the first unnatural structure; a section of wall rising perhaps waist-high, its stones fitted together with such precision that even centuries of weather have failed to separate them. The wall serves no apparent purpose now, standing isolated in the landscape disconnected from any larger structure.

"Chillisar work," Lukkar says, "You'll see plenty more as we go. This whole region was major part of their empire, three hundred years gone now."

Mardonius studies the stonework with renewed interest. The Empire of Chillisar features prominently in military history. It was a vast, sophisticated civilisation that controlled territories from the southern coasts to the Worldspine Mountains before Rande was built on its smouldering ruins; a nation forged by his own ancestors through brutal subjugation. The Eastern Legion's tactical manuals still reference Chillisar formations and strategies, preserved in fragments of texts rescued from their plundered libraries.

As the wagon crests a low rise, the view opens to reveal a landscape dotted with remnants of human endeavour. In a shallow valley to their left a circular arrangement of stones suggests a gathering place or rudimentary fortress. Further west, a square tower stands in improbable isolation, missing its upper third but otherwise intact. Closer to their path, what might have been a roadside shrine has collapsed into a jumble of carved blocks, among which Mardonius glimpses the remains of a statue with a hand still holding what appears to be a sceptre or rod of office.

"Amazing what's survived, isn't it?" Lukkar says, his voice carrying a note of genuine wonder despite what must be long familiarity with these sights. "Even more amazing to think what's been lost."

He gestures toward a particularly intricate section of ruined wall where decorative carvings remain visible: interlacing patterns of leaves and geometric shapes framing what might be stylised human figures.

"They built things to last," Lukkar continues. "Used techniques we can't easily copy even now. That wall there. There's no mortar between those stones. Each one cut to fit its neighbours so perfectly you couldn't slide a knife blade between them. Three centuries of frost and rain and they still stand while our buildings from fifty years ago crumble."

The path bends around a cluster of weathered stones, their inscriptions long since eroded to illegibility. The horse snorts nervously as they pass, perhaps responding to some scent or sound imperceptible to human senses. Lukkar murmurs reassurances, his hand steady on the reins. Akantha's donkey is unmoved.

"This whole area was more densely settled then," he explains. "Villages, trading posts, temples."

As if summoned by his words, the wagon's wheels suddenly transition from rutted dirt to smooth stone. The jolting, creaking progress gives way to almost gliding motion as they pass over a section of ancient roadway partially uncovered by recent rains. The pavers fit together with the same precision as the wall they observed earlier, creating a surface far more even than the maintained roads near Aissentur.

The sensation lasts only moments before they return to the rough dirt track, the contrast making the ordinary path seem even more primitive by comparison. Mardonius finds himself wondering what it would have been like to travel in an age when such engineering was commonplace. When the journey from city to city didn't involve constant jostling and the threat of broken wheels in deep ruts.

"Deeper in those hills," Lukkar says, looking toward the mountain foothills to their north, "are temples and tombs no one's explored. Some say they're full of treasure. Others say they're full of things best left sleeping."

"Fools go looking for Chillisar gold every few years," Lukkar continues. "Most don't come back. Those that do return empty-handed with stories that change depending on how much they've had to drink." He adjusts his position on the bench, leaning forward slightly to ease a cramp. "Strange lights. Moving statues. Voices speaking from empty rooms. The usual nonsense frightened men tell themselves to explain why they ran instead of continuing their search. If you want to explore those places though, you need to do it right."

Mardonius scans the passing landscape with renewed attention. He notices how many of these ruins occupy strategically advantageous locations, hilltops with clear lines of sight, narrows between terrain features that could control passage, elevated positions near water sources. The Chillisar builders understood tactical considerations that remain valid centuries later.

The path curves around a particularly large stand of trees, and Mardonius notices something that a casual observation might miss; subtle rectangular depressions in the earth, partially obscured by scrub and young saplings, but too regular to be natural. Foundations, perhaps, of structures long since collapsed or dismantled for their materials. The trees themselves form too perfect a circle to be random growth which suggests they were planted as boundary markers or windbreaks around a settlement now otherwise gone.

"Most people see only what's still standing," Lukkar says, proving more observant than Mardonius had credited him. "But the real story's in what's hidden. This whole area was built up with scattered structures, their way stations, shrines, watchtowers. The Empire maintained this region as a buffer zone between their core territories and the mountain kingdoms."

Similar to Aissentur's current function, Mardonius reflects, a border settlement maintaining the boundary between distinct powers. History repeats itself in patterns recognisable to those who study it, though the specific actors change.

They pass another section of ancient paved road, this one longer than the last. The wagon's wheels spin almost silently across the smooth surface, the absence of noise making their progress seem temporarily dreamlike. Mardonius feels a strange connection to the countless travellers who must have journeyed this same route centuries before. The merchants with goods to trade, soldiers marching to distant postings, ordinary people moving between settlements now reduced to scattered stones.

"The courier would have aimed to come along this same path." Lukkar points out, "Whatever happened to him happened somewhere between here and Swansbane."

The observation returns Mardonius' focus to their immediate purpose. These ruins have stood for centuries; they'll remain long after this mission is complete. The missing courier presents a more urgent mystery.

"Any particular areas where trouble is more common?" Mardonius asks, his first question in some time.

Lukkar shrugs. "The whole stretch has its dangers, at least up till those foot hills. Bandits sometimes use the ruins for ambush points. Wild animals den in collapsed structures. The usual." He glances at Mardonius. "But once you hit those wooded hills ahead then things get a lot more serious. That's Twisted territory. Lots of nasty man-eaters."

Which suggests the courier met with something unpredictable, Mardonius concludes silently. Rather than a someone specifically waiting for him.

The wagon continues westward, wheels alternating between rutted dirt and occasional stretches of ancient pavement. Behind them, Akantha follows steadily, her eyes constantly scanning the ruins they pass. Mardonius wonders what she sees in these remnants. Is their silent warrior-girl interested in links to a history that predates her tribe or does she see them simply as potential threats to be assessed and avoided.

The sun climbs higher, burning away the last of the morning chill. The Worldspine Mountains now tower over their right rather than ahead of them. The snow-capped and cloud-shrouded peaks are impossibly tall as they gleam in the sunlight. Somewhere ahead of them lies Swansbane and hopefully answers about the missing courier. Behind them stretches a road marked by the rise and fall of powers that once seemed eternal. A physical reminder that all empires eventually become ruins for future travellers to contemplate.

CHAPTER 5

The road narrows as they leave the open plains behind, the wagon's wooden frame protesting each rotation of its wheels across increasingly uneven ground. Mardonius shifts his weight on the hard bench, easing the strain on muscles grown stiff from a whole morning of travel. The landscape has transformed around them as rolling grasslands give way to scattered copses that gradually thicken into proper woodlands, trees closing ranks like silent sentinels along the path. Shadows deepen beneath their spreading branches forming patches of darkness that could hide anything from wild animals to bandits to more unnatural threats.

Mardonius finds his hand drifting closer to his mace, an unconscious adjustment born from years of frontier patrols. His eyes find it hard to rest. They constantly scan the tree line, assessing distances, identifying choke points and potential ambush locations. The wagon slows further as the incline increases, its path now cutting around the first proper hills they've encountered since leaving Aissentur.

"Slow going from here," Lukkar remarks, breaking a silence that had stretched comfortably between them for the past hour. "Road's not maintained like The Mountain Way. Nobody cares much about this stretch except Master Gynn."

To their left, a glint of silver catches Mardonius' eye, it is sunlight reflecting off moving water. The Upper Gift River appears between gaps in the trees, its current flowing westward in a serene manner. The water looks clean and clear, a stark contrast to the muddy streams he'd grown accustomed to during his service in the eastern territories.

"River runs all the way to Swansbane and beyond," Lukkar offers, "Used to be the main trade route centuries back when Chillisar maintained proper ports all along it. Now it's just used by locals for fishing, mostly."

Mardonius studies the waterway with concern. "Deep enough for boats?"

"Small ones, aye. Nothing substantial. Narrows considerably near Swansbane, forms some seriously impressive falls. Not too sure where it leads after that," Lukkar adjusts his grip on the reins, guiding the horse around a particularly deep rut. "The river's not the problem, it is getting down to it that is the issue. From Swansbane it is a steep path."

The trees crowd closer to the road now, their branches occasionally brushing against the canvas covering of the wagon. Mardonius can smell the rich, earthy scent of decomposing leaves mingled with the sharper tang of pine resin. Fresh shoots of green emerge from the forest floor where sunlight manages to pierce the canopy. Spring asserts itself even in these wilder regions, though with less certainty than in the cultivated fields surrounding Aissentur.

"How often do merchants travel this route?" Mardonius asks, more to maintain conversation than from genuine curiosity. It is better to keep Lukkar talking, locals often reveal valuable information without realising it.

"Hardly ever," Lukkar replies with a dismissive wave. "Master Gynn sends a wagon every two weeks. Regular as clockwork, that man. Few independent traders risk it, and those who do usually travel in groups. Not worth the danger for most, when The Mountain Way offers faster and safer prospects."

Mardonius absorbs this information, adding it to his mental map of the region and its dynamics. Isolated routes with limited traffic make ideal hunting grounds for bandits, or worse. Yet Master Gynn maintains regular shipments, suggesting valuable enough trade to justify the risk.

"What makes Swansbane worth the journey?" he asks casually, eyes still tracking the movements among the trees, deer, perhaps, or something less innocent.

Lukkar's weathered face cracks into an unexpected smile, the expression transforming his features from grim determination to almost boyish amusement. "You'll see," he says, cryptic enjoyment evident in his tone. "Best experienced firsthand, Swansbane is."

Mardonius waits for elaboration, but none comes. Lukkar's sudden reticence feels deliberate, as if discussing the settlement might somehow jinx their journey. The wagon driver returns his attention to the road, his previous willingness to share information apparently reaching its limit.

Behind them, Akantha follows with her donkey picking its way carefully along the rutted track. She sits more alert now, Mardonius notices during a backward glance. Her posture remains proudly upright, but her head turns more frequently from side to side, scanning the surrounding woods with the enhanced vigilance of someone accustomed to potential threats.

A sensation has been creeping over Mardonius gradually, the persistent feeling of being observed. It is nothing like the directed scrutiny of an ambush party but something more diffuse and unsettling. The hairs on the back of his neck rise. His skin prickles beneath his leather armour. A soldier's instinct, honed through countless patrols and skirmishes, tells him unseen eyes track their progress through these thickening woods.

He turns his head sharply, following the sensation to a dense patch of undergrowth approximately thirty paces back, where shadow and vegetation form a perfect concealment for... what? Nothing moves there, nothing betrays a presence, yet the feeling persists. He has to fight the urge to string his longbow.

Akantha has stopped her donkey, her head turned toward the same section of forest that drew Mardonius' attention. Her right hand grips her spear tighter, it is not yet raised but clearly at the ready. For a moment, their eyes meet across the distance. He realises this is the only acknowledgment of him she's offered since their journey began. Something flickers in her expression, it is not fear, but more a recognition of shared perception.

"Something watching us?" Mardonius asks Lukkar quietly, his voice pitched to carry no further than the driver's bench.

Lukkar glances around casually, showing none of the focused intensity that has seized his passengers. "Just tricks of the land," he says, waving away their concerns with a flick of his wrist. "These hills play with your mind if you let them. Old places have old shadows."

The wagon creaks onward.

Sunlight filters through the canopy in dappled patterns that shift and move with the breeze, creating an illusion of movement where none exists. Birds call to one another overhead, their communications suddenly ceasing before resuming moments later. The normal rhythms of forest life continue, yet are distorted somehow, as if performing for an audience they've grown accustomed to deceiving.

Mardonius catalogues each detail automatically. No broken branches indicating recent passage. No disturbance in the undergrowth beyond what wind and wildlife might cause. No glint of metal or reflection of eyes from the shadows. Yet the sensation persists – they are not alone in these woods.

The wagon rounds a bend in the road, the tree line receding slightly on their right to reveal a small clearing. Old stumps dot the open space, evidence of human activity in what otherwise feels like wilderness untouched by civilisation. The sensation of being watched fades slightly, though it doesn't disappear entirely.

Mardonius exhales slowly, consciously relaxing muscles that had tensed in preparation for conflict. Beside him, Lukkar hums tunelessly under his breath, seemingly untroubled by the atmosphere that had gripped his passengers. Behind them, Akantha resumes her steady pace, though her vigilance remains heightened and her spear is now held more prominently across her body.

Mardonius is the first to spot it. A splash of unnatural colour against the earthen road ahead. As they draw closer, the wagon slowing naturally on the incline, the disorder resolves into recognisable components. There are scattered white bones, torn strips of leather and fragments of metal from a saddle. It is a horse, or what remains of one. The carcass lies strewn across twenty feet of road, as if something had played with the pieces after stripping the meat clean. The carcass is fresh enough that flies still buzz in interest, yet old enough that most of the flesh has vanished from its exposed bones.

Lukkar brings the wagon to a halt ten paces from the grisly scene. The draft horse snorts nervously, head tossing, nostrils flaring at the scent of death. Mardonius studies the remains with cold assessment, suppressing the revulsion that rises in his throat.

Two days. The courier has been missing only two days, yet the horse's bones lie picked clean. Nature works quickly, but not this quickly. Something unnatural has been at work here.

"This is where your search begins," Lukkar announces, his earlier chattiness giving way to business-like efficiency. He gestures toward the scattered remains.

Mardonius slides from the wagon bench, boots landing with a soft thud on the packed earth. He approaches the remains cautiously, crouching beside what appears to be the largest piece: the horse's skull. Its empty eye sockets staring blankly toward the forest canopy. Teeth still intact. No obvious fracture to the cranium. He shifts his attention to the scattered vertebrae and ribs, noting how widely they're distributed.

No saddlebag. No sign of the brass case Gynn wants recovered.

Movement behind him announces Akantha's approach. She has dismounted from her donkey, the animal tethered loosely to a sapling at the roadside. She carries her spear in her right hand, its butt occasionally striking the ground as she picks her way forward. Her footfalls are nearly silent despite the scattered leaves and twigs, a hunter's tread that speaks of lifelong practice. Unlike Mardonius she wears sandals instead of solid boots.

"No human body," she observes, her first direct words to Mardonius since their journey began. Her voice is lower than he expected, with a melodic quality despite the clipped delivery.

He acknowledges both her observation and the implied question. "Courier might have escaped whatever did this."

Akantha's eyes narrow as she surveys the scene. "Or was taken."

A shiver runs along Mardonius' spine that has nothing to do with the forest's cool shade. He's seen enough battlefields to recognise the implications of a body gone missing. Most natural predators would leave something behind, be it scraps of clothing, broken weapons or perhaps a limb deemed unsuitable for consumption. The absence suggests purpose rather than mere hunger.

Lukkar clears his throat, drawing their attention back to the wagon. "I'll be continuing ahead to Swansbane," he announces. "Master Gynn's goods need delivery, and I make this run alone most times anyway." He adjusts his position on the bench, loosening reins in preparation for departure. "You two follow the trail, see what you can find of our missing courier or his cargo."

Mardonius studies the wagon driver's face, searching for signs of deception or fear. He finds neither, only the weathered impassivity of a man who has travelled dangerous roads for decades and developed a healthy respect for their threats.

"You're leaving us here?" he asks, the question neutral rather than accusatory.

"That's what Master Gynn's paying you for, isn't it?" Lukkar replies. "To find what's missing? Won't find it sitting in my wagon."

Mardonius watches Lukkar. The man has travelled this road many times, claims to make the journey alone regularly, yet shows no hesitation about leaving them to search an area where something has violently destroyed a horse and possibly its rider.

Before he can voice these thoughts, Lukkar leans forward, extending an arm toward him. Mardonius steps closer, expecting a handshake or perhaps a map. Instead, Lukkar's fingers close around his shoulder with unexpected strength, pulling him closer to the wagon.

"Whatever you find, be at Swansbane before dark," Lukkar says, his voice dropping to an urgent murmur. "The gates close at sunset, and you don't want to be outside the walls after nightfall." His fingers tighten momentarily, emphasising each word. "No exceptions. Not for anyone."

The warning echoes their earlier conversation about Swansbane's protocols, but carries new weight given their current surroundings. Mardonius searches Lukkar's eyes, finding no trace of the earlier amusement that had coloured his refusal to discuss the settlement. Now there is only intensity, a sincere urgency that brooks no argument.

"What happens after dark?" Mardonius asks, matching Lukkar's quiet tone.

The wagon driver releases his grip, straightening on the bench. "Just be inside the walls," he repeats, offering no explanation. He underscores his point by looking directly at Akantha, a respectful gesture that she acknowledges with a slight nod. Then he flicks the reins against the draft horse's back, urging the animal forward. The wagon creaks into motion, carefully navigating around the scattered remains before continuing westward along the rutted path. Neither Mardonius nor Akantha speaks as it recedes into the distance, the sound of wheels and hoof beats gradually fading until only forest sounds remain.

CHAPTER 6

The wagon vanishes where the road curves, consumed by the dense woodland. Shadows dance and lengthen under the canopy as a breeze stirs the leaves overhead. Dappled sunlight breaks through in jagged patterns across the rutted path. Despite the movement above, the air hangs thick around them, as if the forest itself holds its breath in anticipation.

Mardonius scans the treeline, his body instinctively shifting to place the scattered horse remains between himself and the deeper shadows of the forest. The early spring sun warms his back through the leather armour, but does nothing to chase away the chill that has settled in his gut. "We need to move quickly," he says, more to break the oppressive silence than because Akantha requires instruction.

She doesn't respond, her attention is already fixed on the grim tableau before them. The horse's remains lie scattered across the rutted track, its bones gleaming unnaturally white against the dark soil. Too clean. Too thoroughly picked. Something hungry passed this way, something with patience and purpose.

Beyond the road, swampy scrubland stretches down towards the gleam of the Upper Gift River, perhaps a hundred feet downslope. Reeds sway in the gentle breeze, creating patterns that could too easily conceal movement. Water birds call to one another in the distance, their cries echoing across the open space.

Mardonius breathes deeply, gathering information from the air itself. The scent is complex; sun-warmed stone and dust from the road, the fetid sweetness of decomposition from the horse remains, and beneath it all, the earthy richness of wet soil and river water. The temperature shifts noticeably as a breeze pushes upward from the riverbank, carrying cooler, damper air that makes the skin on his forearms tighten.

"We could start by examining the immediate area," he suggests, gesturing toward the scattered bones. "Look for signs of..."

"Yes," Akantha interrupts, the single word delivered with such finality that it feels like a complete sentence.

They circle the remains awkwardly, each unsure of the other's methods. Twice they nearly collide when their paths intersect, both stepping back with muttered apologies that sound more like challenges. Mardonius finds himself hyper-aware of her movements, tracking her position even as he searches the ground for clues. Trust doesn't come easily between strangers, especially strangers forced into partnership.

He kneels beside what appears to be the horse's shoulder, a large bone fragment with distinctive tooth marks. His eyes narrow as he examines the patterns, comparing them against mental catalogues compiled through years of frontier skirmishing. Not wolf. Not bear. Something else entirely.

Mardonius investigates methodically, quartering the area around the remains as he would with a Legion search party. He studies the ground with experienced eyes, looking for the tell-tale signs he was trained to recognise: scuffed earth, broken vegetation, discarded items. Five, ten, twenty feet out, in expanding circles. Nothing. The road itself offers little information thanks to its packed surface being resistant to impressions. The surrounding vegetation shows no obvious signs of disturbance.

His jaw tightens with frustration. This isn't right. Something dragged these bones here, or at least scattered them after feeding. There should be tracks, blood trails and at least some indication of movement. Yet he finds nothing but undisturbed forest and road. It's as if the horse materialised here after being stripped of flesh elsewhere.

Ten paces away, Akantha moves differently. Where his search is structured, hers seems almost aimless. She wanders to the edge of the road, then back, her eyes never settling in one place for long. She pauses occasionally to pluck a blade of grass or touch a patch of soil, then continues her seemingly random path.

"Find anything?" he asks, unable to keep the frustration from his voice.

She ignores him, drifting toward the downslope side of the road where the forest gives way to marshy ground. Without warning, she drops to her knees at a patch of mud, her leather armour creaking softly with the movement. Her fingers trace patterns in the wet soil that Mardonius can't discern from his position.

He continues his own search, unwilling to abandon his training despite its apparent failure. The Legion's methods have served him well for a decade, they won't fail him now. Another circuit, another careful examination of the ground, and still nothing. His fingers flex unconsciously in frustration until he forces them to relax.

"Here."

The word is so quiet he almost misses it. Akantha remains kneeling by the mud patch, one finger pointing to depressions in the wet soil. She doesn't look up at him, doesn't gesture for him to approach. Simply points and waits, expecting him to understand.

Mardonius picks his way toward her, careful not to disturb anything that might prove important. When he reaches her side, he sees what she's found. There are faint impressions in the mud, barely visible even from this close. Three elongated depressions, splayed outward like fingers pressed into clay.

"Tracks," he says out of relief more than necessity.

Akantha still refuses to meet his eyes. She gestures farther downslope where more faint depressions form a broken line towards the river.

Mardonius' jaw tightens. He'd missed them completely, too focused on the methodical search patterns that had served him well on firmer ground. The swampy terrain requires different skills he realises. All his training, all his experience, and this tribal girl had found in minutes what he'd failed to see at all.

The objective soldier in him, the one who survived when others didn't, pushes aside the wounded pride. Results matter, not who achieves them.

"Which way?" he asks, deferring to her expertise without hesitation.

Akantha points toward the river. "Go there. We follow" she says and turns toward the downslope path without waiting for his agreement.

Mardonius adjusts his shield strap across his back, ensuring it won't hinder a quick draw if needed. His own armour suddenly feels inadequate against whatever stripped a horse to bones in less than two days. He glances at the sun's position, it is still high enough to provide at least 5 hours of daylight. Remembering Lukkar's warning about reaching Swansbane before dark adds another layer of urgency though.

"We follow," he agrees, and steps after her into the swampy lowland.

The ground changes beneath their feet as they descend toward the riverbank, firm soil gives way to spongy earth that holds a record of their own footprints with ease. Mardonius adjusts his stride choosing shorter steps and more careful placement. Ahead of him, Akantha does the same, moving with her weight distributed perfectly to avoid sinking or creating noise. The air grows heavier with each step downward, moisture clings to his skin and seeps through the seams of his clothing.

The tracks they follow transform as the ground softens. What were mere suggestions in the harder soil above now become definitive impressions. They are elongated footprints with splayed, wide toes that dig deeply into the mud. The stride length alone suggests a creature taller than most men, while the peculiar shape of the foot, if it can even be called that, speaks of something perhaps adapted for both land and water. Certainly nothing human made these marks.

"Getting clearer," Mardonius murmurs, keeping his voice low despite the distance that likely separates them from the tracks' creators.

Akantha doesn't respond verbally but her posture changes subtly. Her shoulders tighten, her grip on her spear shifts to a position that would allow for a quicker thrust. She knows these tracks; the realisation sends a chill through Mardonius. Whatever left these marks is familiar enough to her that mere footprints trigger a combat response.

He studies her reaction more carefully. There is no fear he can detect, or at least, nothing so simple as fear. Instead, her face carries resignation paired with disgust. It is the expression of a warrior who recognises an old enemy rather than a new threat. She catches him watching and holds his gaze as if weighing up whether to share her conclusions. A long breath escapes her, almost a sigh, before she returns her attention to the trail without offering any explanation.

Mardonius doesn't press, she hasn't spoken to him all morning, and she is unlikely to suddenly change now. The information will come when needed and demanding it now would only highlight the fragility of their partnership. Instead, he focuses on their surroundings, cataloguing details that may come in useful later. Reeds rise from the marshy soil in irregular clumps, some nearly as tall as a man. Stunted wide bushes with pale green leaves cluster together in the slightly higher ground. The Upper Gift River itself remains hidden from view but its presence dominates the landscape. It can be heard in the subtle gurgle of moving water, smelled in the distinctive blend of mud and aquatic plants that grows stronger with each step.

Insects buzz around them, small black flies that seem especially attracted to the sweat beading on Mardonius' forehead. He resists the urge to swat them away, unwilling to make unnecessary movements that might give away their position. One lands on his neck, its bite a sharp pinprick that he acknowledges and dismisses in the same moment. Discomfort is temporary, death from carelessness is permanent.

His hand never strays far from the mace hanging at his belt. The weapon's weight is familiar and reassuring. The mace is perfect for the brutal chaos of close combat. Unlike a sword, whose edge can be turned by armour, the mace delivers blunt force that transmits through protection to the flesh and bones beneath. He's crushed skulls with it, shattered limbs, ended threats with the simple physics of weight and velocity. Against an unknown enemy it offers a certainty that edged weapons cannot match.

A sudden sound freezes them both, a splash from somewhere ahead, too large to be made by falling debris or small wildlife. Mardonius drops into a half-crouch, his hand closing around the mace handle without conscious thought. Beside him, Akantha has become utterly still, a statue carved from flesh that happens to hold a spear.

Ten heartbeats pass. Twenty. Nothing further disturbs the ambient sounds of the wetland. Slowly, they straighten and continue forward, but something has changed in their dynamic. Before they moved as separate entities sharing a path, now they unconsciously adjust their positioning to complement each other. Without discussion, Akantha shifts slightly to his left, creating a broader front that would be harder to ambush. Mardonius matches her pace automatically, maintaining the optimal distance for mutual support without hindering each other's weapon arcs.

A bird erupts from a nearby reed patch, its wings beating frantically as it takes flight. Again they freeze, again they wait, again they proceed when no threat materialises. The cycle repeats with each unexpected noise: a branch falling, something slithering through shallow water, the distant call of a water bird. Each false alarm should desensitise them, yet somehow the opposite occurs. Every interruption winds the tension tighter, preparing muscles and reflexes for the moment when the threat proves real.

They push through a particularly dense stand of vegetation, the plants releasing a pungent odour when crushed beneath their feet or brushed aside by their hands. The earthy tang of river water grows stronger but it is accompanied now by another scent, something subtle but unmistakably wrong. Rot, but not the simple decomposition of plants or small animals. Something larger, something with meat and organs that had no business being exposed to air.

Akantha unwinds her sling from her arm bracer with deliberate slowness, careful not to make the leather thong snap or creak. Her free hand dips into the small pouch at her belt, extracting a stone that fits perfectly in her palm. He can see she has chosen well. It is not some rough river rock, but a carefully selected projectile whose surface has been smoothed for accurate flight. The sling itself remains loose in her grip, ready to be loaded and deployed in a single fluid motion that Mardonius suspects she has practiced many thousands of times.

His own shields remains strapped across his back for now, allowing greater manoeuvrability through the thick vegetation. Drawing it would signal his belief that contact was imminent and that is a psychological threshold he's not yet ready to cross. Still, his awareness of its position never wavers, his body is prepared to bring it forward in the same fluid movement that had saved his life countless times on the battlefield.

The tracks continue their relentless path toward the river. Two sets at minimum, possibly three, moving together with purpose. Not hunting – returning. The realisation forms in Mardonius' mind with sudden clarity. These creatures weren't roaming in search of prey; they were returning to their shelter after a successful hunt. The courier's horse had been their target, or at least their victim. And if they took the horse...

"The brass case," he whispers to Akantha. "If they took the courier, they might have taken what he carried."

She nods once, understanding despite the language barrier. Her eyes flick toward the sun, judging its position in the sky, it nears noon. The reminder of Lukkar's warning hangs unspoken between them. Whatever they're going to find, they need to find it quickly. Swansbane's gates will close at sunset, and neither of them wishes to discover first-hand why that rule brooks no exceptions.

The vegetation thins slightly as they approach what appears to be a small clearing near the riverbank. The tracks converge here, becoming a churned mass of footprints that suggests frequent use. Akantha raises her hand, signalling Mardonius to slow his approach. Her head tilts slightly, ears straining for sounds beyond the normal chorus of wetland life.

Twenty feet ahead, the Upper Gift River flows serenely past, its surface occasionally broken by small ripples as fish rise to feed on surface insects. The bank isn't the gradual slope Mardonius expected, but a more defined edge dropping about three feet to the water.

Akantha's free hand gestures toward a large bush growing near the bank, its branches spreading wide enough to provide substantial cover. Her expression remains neutral, but her body tells a different story with muscles coiled tight, weight balanced forward on the balls of her feet, breath controlled and shallow. She's preparing for a fight.

Mardonius follows her cues and sees what caught her attention. Beneath the bush's lower branches, partially obscured by shadow, the ground appears disturbed. Not the random patterns created by animals or weather, but the conscious displacement of soil that suggests purpose. Hands had moved that earth. Or something like hands.

They approach the bush with the careful synchronisation of experienced hunters, each step placed to minimise sound, each movement calculated to maintain maximum awareness of their surroundings. Mardonius circles slightly right while Akantha takes the left, creating a pincer that would catch anything bursting from cover between them. Nothing moves beneath the dense foliage except shadows cast by the noontime sun filtering through leaves. The disturbed earth becomes more visible as they draw closer. It is no certain that this is not some random animal's digging but the intentional construction of something that was meant to remain hidden.

Akantha stops, the tip of her spear indicating a specific point beneath the bush where the soil appears freshly turned. Her nostrils flare slightly, reacting to something Mardonius can't yet detect. She makes a subtle gesture with her free hand: two fingers pointing toward her eyes, then toward the ground. Look closer.

Mardonius approaches with his mace drawn, ready to swing at the first sign of threat. He crouches beside the bush, muscles tensed for an immediate jump back if necessary. The branches are thick enough to require both hands to move them aside, so he reluctantly places his weapon on the ground, trusting Akantha to provide cover. Thick leaves brush against his face as he pushes into the vegetation, their undersides damp with moisture that smears across his cheek.

The branches part to reveal what the bush has been concealing. It is a hole in the ground, roughly three feet in diameter, its edges too perfectly circular to be natural. The sides appear smooth, tamped down by frequent use and descending at an angle into darkness that his eyes can't penetrate. The entrance to a tunnel, or perhaps a burrow, large enough for a man to enter if he were willing to crouch.

Then the smell hits him.

Mardonius jerks back instinctively, unable to prevent the grimace that twists his features. The stench claws its way into his nostrils and clings there, a miasma of rot and filth so concentrated it feels almost solid. River mud forms the base notes, but layered above it are the unmistakable odours of decaying flesh, old blood and something else, the acrid, almost chemical scent that he associates with the Twisted creatures he's encountered on the eastern frontier. His stomach clenches tight, fighting the natural urge to empty itself.

"Hsst," Akantha warns, her body shifting into a more defensive stance, spear angled toward the hole. She's smelled it too but shows less reaction, as if she expected this particular offense to her senses.

Water drips somewhere in the darkness below, the sound echoing strangely as if traveling through multiple connected chambers. The droplets strike with irregular rhythm – plip... plip... plip-plip – creating an effect more disconcerting than simple white noise. In his mind's eyes he pictures something moving down there, disturbing the water's surface. Waiting.

Mardonius takes up his mace again. His thumb traces the familiar groove worn into the handle from years of identical grip, the wood smooth and responsive against his callused skin.

"Fisher Folk," Akantha says flatly, actually volunteering information without being directly questioned. The words fall between them like stones dropped into still water, creating ripples of understanding. "Twisted creatures."

The term crystallises into fragments of stories Mardonius has heard during his service. Villagers telling tales of pale, unnaturally thin beings that haunt waterways with limbs elongated beyond human proportion, and their bodies adapted for both land and water. They are said to ambush settlements at night, killing the men and taking off with the women.

"How many, do you think?" he asks, voice pitched low enough that it won't carry down the tunnel.

Akantha considers the tracks they followed, her eyes narrowing slightly with the effort of calculation. "Two or three," she replies. "Not a full nest." The relief in her voice is subtle but unmistakable. A small group, then, dangerous but manageable with proper tactics.

Mardonius unslings his shield from across his back, sliding his left arm through the securing straps, its weight settles reassuringly against his forearm. In close quarters a shield is as much a weapon as protection, its edge and face are capable of stunning or disabling opponents in the confined space of the tunnel. For now though he uses it to clear the overhanging branches from over the hole.

"They will have weapons," Akantha adds, her eyes never leaving the dark opening. Her expression hardens. "They eat humans."

The statement requires no elaboration. The missing courier's fate becomes clearer, though Mardonius still holds hope that the man somehow escaped or hid elsewhere. But if these creatures took the horse, they likely took its rider as well, and with him, the brass case Master Gynn wants recovered.

"We'll need light down there," Mardonius says, mentally calculating the tunnel's dimensions against his own. He can fit, but movement will be restricted and their fighting stance compromised. Hardly ideal conditions for combat, especially against creatures adapted to such environments.

Akantha waves her arm around at the bushes and shrubs that make up the vegetation this side of the road. "We can make a torch."

They lock eyes and for once neither of them avoid it. Each recognises something shifted between them now they face a common threat together. His Royal Army discipline and her Takaz'Ran ferocity suddenly feel like two sides of the same coin. He notices that even

Akantha's stance has changed with her shoulder angling towards him rather than away.

"They might sleep," she says, her voice betraying a hint of uncertainty. "Daylight makes them slow."

Mardonius glances at the sun's position again. Whatever they do, they must do it quickly.

"The brass case," he reminds her. "Find it and get out. No unnecessary risks."

CHAPTER 7

The stench from the hole lingers in Mardonius' nostrils, a miasma that coats his throat and settles in his lungs like liquid dread. He steps back from the half-cleared bush, creating distance from the entrance without retreating completely.

The strong noon sun still bathes the riverbank in deceptive warmth, casting dappled shadows through the leaves that dance across the disturbed earth surrounding the lair's entrance. Such ordinary light seems wrong, somehow, now that they know what waits beneath.

Akantha turns away from the hole and she crosses back toward where her donkey waits. The animal stands patiently beside a cluster of reeds, ears flicking occasionally at insects that buzz too close. Its eyes follow her approach with the calm trust of a beast that has known only kindness from its master.

"Must secure Fer," she says over her shoulder, her voice carries none of the sharpness she typically directs at Mardonius.

She leads the donkey toward a sturdy bush several paces from the tunnel entrance, its branches thick enough to hold the animal if it panics. Her hands work the reins with ease, creating a secure knot that will release quickly if pulled from the proper angle. Throughout this process, her attention never fully leaves the hole in the ground, her body positioned to react to any threat that might emerge from below.

With the donkey secured, Akantha's demeanour transforms. Her perpetually tight shoulders soften slightly as she strokes the animal's muzzle, her fingers tracing the lines of its face with genuine affection. She leans close, pressing her forehead briefly against the donkey's, murmuring words in her native tongue. The language sounds ancient, containing rhythms and tones that modern Randeri speech lacks entirely.

Mardonius catches the name "Eanna" repeated several times, the familiar deity's name standing out amid the foreign words. A prayer for protection, perhaps? Asking the warrior goddess to watch over this loyal beast while they venture below. The contrast between her tenderness toward the animal and her coldness toward him strikes Mardonius as oddly revealing. It is as if the capacity for connection exists within her but has been forcibly withheld from human interaction.

The donkey nudges against her hand, seeking more attention. She obliges briefly before straightening, the warriors mask sliding back into place as she turns toward Mardonius.

"Need light," she states, scanning the vegetation around them. "Torch."

Mardonius has already assessing the available materials. "Dry reeds for the core. Green branches to shape it. We'll need something to bind them."

"Long grass there," Akantha points toward a patch of tall, fibrous plants growing near the water's edge. "Strong enough."

They work in parallel rather than together, each gathering materials from different areas to maximise their efforts. Mardonius strips the outer layers from reeds, collecting the dry interior pulp that will catch flame most readily. The texture is surprisingly silky between his fingers, the plant's inner structure revealing itself as a perfect tinder. Akantha harvests grasses and twists them into crude but effective rope, her fingers working with the speed and certainty of someone who has made such bindings hundreds of times before.

The sun is a constant reminder of their need for haste. Mardonius feels each passing moment as a physical weight pressing against his shoulders. Lukkar's warning echoes in his mind – be inside Swansbane's walls before dark, no exceptions.

"They be Fisher Folk," Akantha suddenly states as she pauses in her twisting of grass fibres. "Our people fought them and passed down warning of their ways. They raided river camp." Her fingers resume their work. "Took two women."

The matter-of-fact delivery impacts Mardonius more than any graphic description might have. He continues wrapping dry plant material around a straight branch, binding it as tightly as possible with the twisted grass Akantha has provided to force the fuel to burn longer rather than brighter. The torch takes shape beneath his hands, crude but functional.

"Tell me about them," he says, keeping his tone conversational. "I need to know what we're facing."

Akantha secures the bindings for the outer layer of their torch with a complex knot before responding. "Tall. Thin like stretched hide. Skin white where sun doesn't burn it." Her words come carefully, it feels like she is reciting passed down knowledge rather than speaking from experience. "Hands webbed. Feet too. Long arms, longer legs." She demonstrates the proportions by holding her own arm at an exaggerated length.

"Good swimmers?"

"Very. Better than any human." She tests her handiwork's construction, squeezing it to ensure the binding holds. "They drag prey underwater. Drown it first, then feed." A shadow crosses her face, some private horror glimpsed and quickly suppressed. "They work together. Like to ambush not fight."

Mardonius mentally catalogues these details against his own tactical experience. "Weapons?"

"Spears. Nets." She taps her own spear lying beside her. "Not as good made as ours. But good enough."

"I'd always assumed they were just an old wives' tale," Mardonius admits.

Akantha studies him for a moment, perhaps reassessing him based on this confession of ignorance. "They love water. Need it. Stay near rivers, lakes." She points toward the tunnel entrance. "Build these paths to water. Come out at night to hunt."

Something in her delivery suggests gaps in her knowledge, there are certainties mixed with suppositions, rumours as yet untested. She speaks with the conviction of someone who knows of these creatures but lacks the comprehensive understanding that comes from prolonged study.

"Will the torch hurt them?" Mardonius asks, hefting their completed creation. The tightly bundled reeds feel substantial in his hand but nowhere near as good as a lantern or pitch torch. If only they had some oil to douse the flammable core.

"They see in dark. Eyes big." She cups her hands around her own eyes to illustrate. "Light pains them. Makes them hurt." A pause, then a confession of her own, "At least, that's what the songsmith says."

Mardonius hefts the makeshift torch, estimating its burn time to be fifteen minutes, twenty at most. Not nearly enough to explore whatever warren might sprawl beneath them. With luck, the pitiful flame might blind the creatures momentarily, a fleeting edge against things born to darkness.

"It's not much," he says, eyeing their creation critically.

"It's what we have," Akantha replies, the practicality in her voice matching his own pragmatism. She takes the torch from Mardonius, "Better than nothing."

She rises to her feet, torch in one hand, spear in the other, her posture communicating readiness despite the uncertain nature of what awaits them. For the first time since their journey began, Mardonius sees something beyond cold competence in her bearing – a fierce determination that mirrors his own approach to impossible tasks. They may come from different worlds, follow different paths, but the warrior's code transcends such boundaries.

The stench from the hole seems to have intensified, as if the creatures below sense their coming. Mardonius takes his Ring Mail armour from his backpack. Carefully removing it from its oiled cloth cover he slips it over his leather armour to provide an essential extra layer of protection. It might be expensive as hell to repair but this is a time where its extra protection is worth it.

Mardonius crouches beside the hole, measuring its dimensions against his own frame. The circular opening descends at a steep angle before disappearing into absolute darkness, its walls packed smooth from the passage of creatures unsuited for daylight. He traces the edge with calloused fingers, feeling the transition from sun-warmed surface soil to the perpetually damp earth below; a physical threshold between their world and whatever waits beneath.

"Tight space," he observes, sitting back on his heels. "We'll need to move carefully. Single file."

Akantha's eyes narrow as she conducts her own assessment. "You first or me?"

Mardonius considers the question, weighing tactical advantages against the unknown layout awaiting them. His mind slips effortlessly into the familiar patterns of military planning, breaking the problem into components that can be solved methodically.

"I'll take point," he decides. "Shield forward, you behind with spear and torch." He demonstrates the formation with his hands, one cupped to represent his shield, the other extended to mimic her spear reaching past him. "Like a shield wall, an army formation. I block, you strike. Anything gets vulnerable or too close I will have my mace."

He expects resistance or at least debate from the proud Takaz'Ran woman, but Akantha's agreement comes with surprising speed. "Good plan. Shield protects torch too." She tests the balance of her spear against the weight of the unlit torch in her other hand. "You know this fighting?"

"Ten years in the Army," he confirms, the admission slipping out before he can consider its implications. "Shield wall tactics are standard against equal numbers or in confined spaces."

There is a subtle shift in Akantha's attitude towards him at this, as her previous dismissal of him softens into a more accurate assessment. For warriors facing imminent danger, relevant skills outweigh personal antipathies. Perhaps Mardonius is not the only one to underestimate his companion.

"We need rope," she says, scanning the vicinity. "For climbing back if needed." She walks over to her donkey's bags and retrieves a coil of weathered but serviceable rope, brought along for precisely such contingencies.

The material feels rough against Mardonius' palms as he tests its strength, the fibres resist his attempt to fray them. He searches the clearing for a suitable anchor point, eventually selecting a massive exposed tree root that curves from the soil like a petrified serpent.

Working together without discussion, they secure one end of the rope around the root with a series of interlocking knots. Each contributes techniques from different traditions that nonetheless complement each other. Her knowledge of bindings that resist water's interference, his expertise in knots that distribute weight evenly across fibre. The finished anchor point would satisfy the most demanding Legion officer.

"Ready for light?" he asks, reaching for the flint and steel pouch at his belt.

Akantha positions herself beside him, holding their torch at the perfect angle for ignition. The fluidity of their coordination belies their previous awkwardness as the immediacy of danger begins the difficult task of forging a functional partnership.

The flint strikes steel with a familiar scraping sound, sparks flying toward the dry material. Three attempts yield nothing but momentary glimmers that die before catching. On the fourth strike, a tiny ember takes hold in the reed pulp. Mardonius cups his hand around this fragile beginning, sheltering it from the breeze while Akantha leans down to add her careful breath. The ember grows, consuming surrounding fibres until flames appear, tentative at first, then with increasing confidence. It sputters to life, bathing their faces in wavering orange light that transforms their features into something ancient and elemental. Shadows dance across Akantha's face, emphasising the sharp lines of her cheekbones and turning her eyes into bottomless pools. Her expression remains focused, betraying neither fear nor excitement as she adjusts her grip on the newly burning torch.

The flame paints their surroundings with its inconsistent illumination, transforming the ordinary riverbank into something mythic and potentially treacherous. Shadows stretch and contract with each fluctuation of the fire, creating the illusion of movement where none exists. The torch's light clarifies their immediate vicinity while simultaneously deepening the darkness beyond its reach, as if drawing a boundary between safety and peril.

Smoke curls upward from the burning reeds, carrying a pungent odour that temporarily masks the stench from the hole. The flame itself provides less illumination than Mardonius had hoped, just a sickly orange glow that barely penetrates three feet in any direction. It will be enough to navigate by, perhaps enough to temporarily blind creatures accustomed to perfect darkness, but little more.

Mardonius conducts a final equipment check as a matter of course, each movement burned into muscle memory through thousands of repetitions. Shield secured but positioned for quick deployment. Mace hanging from his belt. Water skin half-full, secured tightly to prevent sloshing noises. Every item in its place, ready for the moment when seconds will determine survival.

He meets Akantha's eyes across the wavering torch flame, seeking confirmation of her readiness.

"Remember," he says, unable to resist a final instruction, "We find the case and get out. No heroics."

"No hero," she agrees.

Mardonius positions himself at the hole's edge, legs dangling into darkness, the rope gripped firmly in his left hand. His shield remains strapped across his back for now, creating a momentary vulnerability that his training screams against but there's no alternative, the descent requires both hands and Akantha needs both of hers for the torch and her spear.

He lowers himself slowly into the opening, feeling the temperature drop with each hands-breadth of descent. The packed earth walls press close against his shoulders threatening to trap him if he makes a wrong movement. The smell intensifies as he drops deeper, assaulting his senses with multiple layers of wrongness, the river mud and decay intertwined with that distinctive chemical odour that marks creatures touched by whatever foul force created them.

The tunnel angles downward at roughly forty-five degrees and is much steeper than it appeared from above. His boots scrabble for purchase against the smooth walls, finding occasional protrusions that serve as footholds. The rope creaks with his weight, the sound amplified by the confined space until it seems to shout their presence to anything waiting below.

Eight or nine feet down his boots finally hit the floor. The tunnel levels here slightly before bending to the right, disappearing around a curve that conceals whatever lies beyond. Water glistens on the walls here, seeping through from the nearby river. The air feels thick and oppressive, laden with moisture and the accumulated breath of creatures that have passed this way before him.

He pauses at this junction, one hand maintaining a secure grip on the rope while the other reaches for his mace. Above him, Akantha's form blocks most of the natural light from the entrance, her silhouette rimmed with afternoon sun. The torch in her hand creates a halo effect around her head as she prepares to follow his descent, her expression is hidden in shadow but her posture communicates tense readiness.

"See anything?" she whispers, her voice barely audible yet still somehow too loud in this unnatural passageway.

"Tunnel bends ahead," he replies at the same volume. "And also goes straight behind but sounds like it ends at the water that way. Wait until I'm clear before you come down."

Mardonius releases the rope. He presses back against the wall of the tunnel while his boots find secure footing.

The position is awkward but stable but it allows him to unstrap his shield and position it before him.

The torch descends behind him as Akantha navigates the same narrow drop. The wavering light creates intense highlights as well as dark shadow shapes on the tunnel walls. The flames reflect off the moisture, transforming ordinary water droplets into gleaming eyes that seem to watch their progress with malevolent anticipation.

CHAPTER 8

The tunnel constricts around them like a throat swallowing prey, the packed earth walls pressing against Mardonius' shoulders as he steadies himself at the bend. The air hangs heavy with decay and river mud, each breath coating his lungs with the unmistakable signature of the Twisted.

"Hold," Akantha whispers close to his ear, her voice barely audible over the soft dripping of water. "Need to check behind."

The passage behind them stretches straight toward what must be an underwater entrance from the river. Akantha crouches at the junction, holding the torch low to examine the ground. Tiny ripples disturb the shallow water pooling where the tunnel floor dips slightly. The surface reflects fractured light back at her, creating patterns that shift and reform with hypnotic rhythm.

"River comes in here when higher," she confirms, pointing to a water line stained along the walls about a foot above the current level. "They swim in, climb up." Her finger traces the path a Fisher Folk might take, from water to tunnel to whatever awaits them ahead.

Mardonius studies the construction of the tunnel while she investigates. It is not natural, no cave formation creates passages this uniform. The walls have been deliberately excavated, packed smooth by hands or tools. Occasional roots protrude through the ceiling, these intrusions have been carefully trimmed rather than removed completely thus maintaining the structural integrity of the earthen ceiling.

Small niches appear at irregular intervals along the walls, each containing objects whose purpose he can only guess at. A collection of smooth river stones arranged in a pattern that might be meaningful or random. Fragments of bone, some recognisably animal, others disturbingly human-like in their proportions. Tufts of dried plant matter bundled and secured with what appears to be sinew. Everything carries the patina of regular handling, nothing is dusty or looks forgotten.

"Definitely inhabited," he concludes, keeping his voice low.

Akantha returns to his side, "Certain now, Fisher Folk territory." Her eyes scanning the dark bend in front of them, "Smell stronger ahead."

She's right. The fetid odour intensifies with each step deeper into the earth. It clings to the back of Mardonius' throat, making each breath a conscious effort.

The tunnel narrows further beyond the bend, forcing them to adjust their formation. Mardonius tests the width with his shield, finding barely enough space to manoeuvre properly.

"Too tight for proper swing," he mutters, testing the arc needed for his mace against the available space. His weapon requires room to build momentum, in these confines, its effectiveness will be significantly reduced.

"I stay close," Akantha assures him, adjusting her grip on both torch and spear. "Light high, spear ready."

Mardonius notes how she's modified her stance. She holds the makeshift torch in the same hand that has her small buckler strapped to it. Her spear arm is free for thrusting attacks which require less space than his mace. The arrangement is awkward but functional. He sees evidence of her quick adaptation to changing circumstances and she is obviously used to working as part of a team. These are excellent traits in a combat partner and ones he tried hard to drill in to the young headstrong soldiers he used to command.

They proceed cautiously down a steepening slope, each step placed with full awareness to minimise noise and ensure solid footing in the damp earth. Mardonius leads with his shield raised, creating a protective barrier behind which both can shelter if needed. The passage curves slightly leftward, preventing them from seeing more than a few feet ahead at any given moment. The torchlight throws their shadows against the walls, distorted shapes that seem to move independently of their bodies.

Water seeps from the ceiling in places, forming droplets that fall with irregular percussion against the tunnel floor. Each impact sounds unnaturally loud in the confined space, like fingers tapping to gain attention. The air grows thicker, harder to breathe, as if reluctant to enter their lungs.

A few minutes of cautious progress brings them to another slight bend, this time to the right. Mardonius pauses, raising his hand in the universal signal for silence. Something has changed in the quality of the air. There is a subtle shift in pressure that suggests a larger space ahead. He strains his ears, filtering out the sound of their breathing and the persistent dripping of water. Nothing. No movement. No voices. No scrape of weapons being readied. Just the weighted silence of a space that feels inhabited despite its apparent emptiness.

The hairs on the back of his neck rise, an animal response to unseen threat. It is not fear, soldiers who survive a decade of service learn to transmute fear into something more useful. This sensation is the body's recognition of imminent danger, a warning system far more reliable than conscious thought.

"Feel it?" Akantha whispers, her breath warm against his ear as she leans close to avoid being overheard.

She feels it too then, that electric prickling that precedes violence. Her voice reveals none of the earlier resignation that had coloured her response to discovering Fisher Folk tracks. Now her expression is that of a predator rather than prey.

The torch flickers alarmingly, the flame shrinking as it consumes the outer layer of its tightly bound fuel. He fears they have perhaps ten minutes of light remaining. The knowledge adds urgency to their mission. They must find the brass case quickly or abandon the search entirely.

"Forward," he decides, voice barely audible. "Slowly."

Akantha's says nothing but shadows his steps onward. There is no retreat now, there is only the path ahead and whatever waits around the bend. The torch sputters once, as if in protest, before steadying again with a renewed determination that matches their own.

The screech hits them like a physical blow. It was a sound no human throat could produce; high-pitched yet guttural, the cry of something that did not belong in this world. It reverberates through the tunnel, bouncing off the damp walls and multiplying until it seems to come from everywhere at once. Mardonius instinctively drops lower behind his shield, muscles tensing for the attack that inevitably follows such a warning.

"They know," Akantha hisses, pressing closer behind him, the torch raised higher to illuminate whatever might emerge from the darkness ahead.

The corridor widens slightly around the bend, offering a tantalising glimpse of a larger chamber beyond. The torchlight reaches just far enough to show the continuation of the tunnel but fails to penetrate the deeper shadows from where the screeching originated. Mardonius narrows his eyes, trying to discern movement in the gloom, when something whistles through the air toward them.

A net flies from the darkness, its weighted edges spinning outward to expand its reach. Mardonius raises his shield instinctively, but the projectile never reaches them. Instead, it catches on a protruding tree root above their heads, the weights wrapping around the gnarled wood with a series of dull thuds. The net hangs there, swaying slightly, its crude construction revealed in the torchlight, just rough fibres woven in irregular patterns, edges weighted with stones wrapped in some kind of animal skin.

"Waste of a good ambush." Mardonius mutters even as his pulse quickens. The failed attack reveals crucial information: their opponents aren't particularly skilled with their weapons, but more importantly, they've confirmed their presence without him even seeing them.

The momentary relief evaporates as another screech erupts from the darkness. This time it is joined by a second voice, one that is deeper and more resonant. At least two attackers are confirmed now. Mardonius catches a flicker of movement beyond the torchlight's reach, of something pale sliding between deeper shadows.

"Ready," he warns Akantha, bracing for another attack.

It comes immediately. It is another net spinning toward them from a slightly different angle than the first. This one flies true, with no convenient root to intercept its path. Mardonius pivots to block but his timing is off by crucial fractions of a second. The net engulfs his right side, tangling his mace arm and wrapping around the edge of his shield. The weights swing around, smacking against his armour with dull impacts, further entangling him in the fibrous mesh.

"No!" he grunts, instinctively trying to swing his mace free only to find the weapon hopelessly enmeshed in the clinging fibres. With the choice being shield or mace he drops the mace onto to the muddy tunnel floor, as close to his feet as he can make it.

Mardonius keeps his shield raised with his left arm, maintaining their primary defence even as his right hand works frantically to free itself from the clinging mesh.

"Knife," Akantha suggests urgently.

Before he can explain that he has no dagger to draw a crude spear thrusts out from the darkness, aiming for the gap between the corridor and the raised shield. The attack is hasty and poorly aimed causing the spear point to skitter across the tunnel wall a foot to his left. The weapon withdraws immediately, leaving a scratch in the packed earth.

Akantha responds instantly, lunging her own spear past Mardonius' right side. The movement is fluid and steady, the weapon an extension of her arm as she thrusts toward their unseen attacker. Unfortunately the angle is awkward, constrained by the tunnel's dimensions and Mardonius' entangled position. Her spear point catches in the hanging net, twisting its course sideways and throwing her off balance.

Something pulls the weapon sharply from the darkness, it is not the creature itself but the net being yanked violently backward. The sudden force tears Akantha's spear from her grasp, the weapon falling to the floor in the gloom beyond the torchlight's reach. She curses in her native tongue but Mardonius gets the gist of it.

"Hold the light higher," Mardonius orders, still struggling with the net entangling his arm. His fingers work carefully despite the urgency, searching for key junction points in the mesh where a single strand's removal will loosen entire sections. The weights continue to hinder him, swinging with each movement and creating new tangles even as he undoes others.

Akantha raises the torch, stretching her arm to maximum extension. The flame gutters dangerously, threatening to extinguish itself before rallying with renewed brightness. The improved illumination pushes back the darkness another few feet, revealing more of the tunnel ahead but still nothing of their attackers.

Two spears thrust from the shadows simultaneously, a coordinated attack from different heights. The lower one aims for Mardonius' legs while the higher targets his chest. In the improved light, he catches glimpse of what guides one of the weapons - a pale, unnaturally elongated arm extending from darkness, fingers webbed and glistening with moisture. The sight is so alien, so wrong in its proportions, that for an instant he falters.

Training reasserts itself immediately. He drops his stance, allowing the higher spear to pass over his shield while the lower scrapes harmlessly against its metal face. The shield deflection forces this second spear downward, its crude point stabbing into the tunnel floor where it lodges in the mud.

"The lower," Akantha calls, having spotted something he missed. "Weak grip!"

Mardonius leverages his shield against the lodged spear, pressing down with even force. The poorly made weapon snaps with a sharp crack, leaving its hidden wielder holding a useless shaft while the point remains embedded in the ground.

His right hand finally works free of the entangling net, the last weighted corner falling away as he tears through a crucial knot. Immediately he crouches, fingers finding his mace on the tunnel floor, the familiar weight returning to his palm like a missing piece restored. The net still clings to portions of his shield, but his weapon arm is free, and that makes all the difference.

"Can't reach spear," Akantha urges, keeping the torch held high while her right foot pats the floor where her weapon should be. The tunnel's confines leave her no certain path to retrieve it.

"Forward," she demands, her voice tight with controlled tension. "They have advantage at distance."

Mardonius hesitates for only a moment. Advancing means committing fully to the fight and abandoning the relative safety of their defensive position, but she's right, their opponents have the reach advantage with their spears. His mace requires closer quarters to be effective. With one of the enemies' spears broken and their nets expended, the tactical calculus has shifted.

"Stay behind our shield," he insists, tightening his grip on the mace. "Ready... Now go!"

With a deep breath that fills his lungs with the fetid air, he pushes forward into the gloom beyond the bend, shield leading their advance toward whatever pale horrors wait in the darkness.

Mardonius advances with his shield forward and mace held defensively. He will use the metal-reinforced edge to ward off any further attacks rather than committing to full swings in the constricted space. The tunnel widens incrementally with each step, the packed earth walls receding just enough to allow his arms more freedom. Behind him, Akantha keeps pace, the torch's flame casting their shadows before them like heralds announcing their approach to the waiting darkness.

The broken spear shaft still protrudes from the tunnel floor, creating an obstacle they carefully navigate over. As they pass it, Akantha spots her own spear lying where it fell after being yanked from her grip. She stoops quickly, fingers closing around the familiar wooden shaft, her movements so fluid they barely interrupt their forward progress. The weapon returns to her hand to her obvious relief, her posture straightening with renewed confidence.

"Better," she murmurs, adjusting her grip to maintain both spear and torch in workable positions.

A sudden sound erupts from ahead but not like the earlier screech. It is instead a wet thud followed by frantic scrabbling. Something heavy has fallen, its impact followed by desperate attempts to regain footing. Mardonius recognises the sounds of combat advantage, one of their opponents is temporarily vulnerable and struggling to recover position.

"One down," he says quietly, increasing their pace slightly to capitalise on the moment.

Before they can advance further, the second Fisher Folk bursts from the shadows with explosive force. It launches itself toward them like something propelled by unnatural energies, a pale blur resolving into horrifying clarity as it enters the torchlight.

The creature stands nearly seven feet tall, its body a grotesque study in wrongness. Limbs extend far beyond human proportions with arms hanging almost to the floor whilst being still bent at the elbow. Its skin glistens with a slick, translucent quality that reveals shadowy suggestions of organs beneath. The face stretches too long, with everything compressed into the lower third as if its skull continued growing after its features had set. The eyes bulge unnaturally large, its pupils expanded to consume nearly all the whites as they reflect the torchlight with an oily sheen.

The Fisher Folk's jaw hinges open wider than seems structurally possible, revealing rows of small, needlelike teeth set in gums that appear raw and inflamed. Its chest heaves with laboured breathing with the ribcage visible through skin stretched thin across its frame. The stench that emanates from it, that distinctive chemical reek present to a lesser or greater degree in all the Twisted, intensifies to nearly unbearable levels in its immediate presence.

It screeches again, the sound erupting from that impossible mouth with enough force to spray droplets of saliva against Mardonius' shield. It is not reaching for him though, its impossibly long arms extend toward Akantha, webbed fingers splayed to grasp and capture.

Mardonius reacts with instincts honed through countless border skirmishes. He pivots slightly, angling his shield to intercept the creature's reaching arms even as he pushes outward. The manoeuvre catches the Fisher Folk mid-lunge, deflecting its momentum toward the tunnel wall instead of Akantha. Those elongated limbs, advantages in water, become liabilities in a confined space, they are easily overextended and difficult to retract quickly.

The creature slams against the packed earth with enough force to dislodge small clumps of dirt from the ceiling. It crumples momentarily, its awkward proportions folding like a dropped marionette as it slides to the tunnel floor.

"Advancing!" Mardonius calls, not waiting to see if the creature recovers. Tactical assessment demands they press their advantage, he must find the second opponent before the first regains its footing. This means trusting Akantha to handle the downed enemy.

Three more strides bring him into a space that suddenly opens wider. it is not quite a proper chamber but it is a significant expansion of the tunnel into what must serve as living quarters. The ceiling rises a full foot higher, while the walls pull back to create an area he guesses to be about twelve feet in diameter. The floor dips slightly toward the centre, creating a shallow depression filled with mud of an almost fluid consistency. It is dark here, the torch's light struggles to illuminate this space.

Mardonius spots the second Fisher Folk across this space, its tall form unfolding from where it had slipped and fallen. This one differs from the other. It is smaller, with a frame that suggests female morphology despite its alien nature. As it straightens, he sees confirmation in two rows of sagging breasts that hang from its chest like withered fruit, their purpose as disturbing as their appearance.

He moves to attack, pushing off hard from the tunnel entrance toward this new threat, but his boot finds no purchase on the slick mud floor. His forward drive betrays him, sending him sliding awkwardly, arms windmilling to maintain balance. The Fisher Folk female sees his vulnerability and thrusts forward with her crude spear, the weapon being little more than a sharpened stick hardened by fire.

Despite his precarious footing, Mardonius manages to sidestep the thrust, allowing the spear to pass harmlessly to his left. He uses the movement to continue his advance, closing the distance until he's within arm's reach of the creature. His shield comes up and forward in a well-drilled motion, the metal-reinforced edge catching the Fisher Folk under what passes for her chin, driving it backward until its spine meets the earthen wall.

In the close quarter's melee, with the creature pinned, he notices two small forms lying in the mud near his feet. Infant Fisher Folk, their proportions even more disturbing in miniature. They already have limbs too long for their torsos and bulbous heads but their large eyes are sealed shut. They wriggle in the mud, making high-pitched mewling sounds that scrape against his eardrums.

The female responds to their cries, fighting against Mardonius' shield with renewed energy. She manages to work her spear into position for another thrust but the angle is awkward and constrained by his pressure against her body. The attack is weak and easily deflected by a slight adjustment of his shield.

Mardonius counters immediately, his mace swinging in an upward arc that connects with the Fisher Folk's shoulder. Bone gives way beneath the impact with a wet crunch and the creatures scream shifts pitch to something almost human in its pain. He pulls his shield back causing the female to fall forward slightly which allows him to follow through with a second blow targeted at the elongated head. The mace catches the Fisher Folk on its temple, the impact drives its skull back against the packed earth wall with devastating force.

The creature goes limp instantly, unconscious or dead. Mardonius doesn't pause to determine which, the immediate threat neutralised, he spins back toward the tunnel entrance, where Akantha faces the first and larger Fisher Folk alone.

"Akantha!" he calls, already moving to assist, boots finding better purchase now that he anticipates the treacherous footing.

Akantha stands her ground as the larger Fisher Folk struggles to its feet, its limbs unfolding in a motion that defies natural movement. Her spear is already in motion before the creature fully rises, the thrust driving the point deep into the pallid flesh where a human's lung would be. Impact jolts through her arms, the sensation not of piercing muscle and sinew but of puncturing something with the consistency of wet paper.

The Fisher Folk screeches and recoils, elongated fingers clutching at the wound as Akantha withdraws her weapon with a vicious twist. Blood follows the spearhead's exit, but it is nothing like the crimson rush of human injury. Instead, a thin, watery fluid seeps from the puncture, its colour a sickly yellow-white that catches the torchlight with an oily sheen.

The smell hits immediately, not the metallic tang of normal blood but something wrong, like spoiled milk mixed with the caustic bite of urine left too long in the sun. Akantha turns her face away instinctively, fighting the urge to gag as the odour fills the confined space.

The Fisher Folk straightens despite its injury. Its wound is already congealing in a way no human's would. It towers over Akantha, those impossible limbs unfolding to their full extension as it prepares another attack. She thrusts again with her spear but this time the creature is ready, its body twisting with unnatural flexibility to avoid the point.

Akantha's eyes narrow as she reassesses her weapon choice. The spear, ideal for the tunnel's approach, proves less effective now that the Fisher Folk is close. Its reach exceeds her own, and its flexibility negates the advantage of the spear's length. In these closer quarters, with the wounded creature alert to her attacks, she needs something else.

Her decision formed in an instant, she drops the spear, letting it clatter to the ground as her hand moves to the bone-handled knife at her belt. The weapon slides free with a soft whisper of leather, blade catching the torchlight with a hungry gleam. The dagger is clearly superior craftsmanship to anything the Fisher Folk possess, a proper fighting tool rather than a desperate modification of everyday implements.

The Fisher Folk seizes the moment of transition, lunging forward while she's between weapons. Its elongated arm extends with whip-like speed, webbed fingers formed into a fist that connects with Akantha's upper arm. The impact spins her half around, the blow carrying much more force than the creature's wasted frame suggests possible.

Pain flashes across Akantha's face but she uses her rotational momentum to advantage. She pivots completely, transforming the defensive motion into an offensive one, bringing her dagger around in a tight arc that terminates in the Fisher Folk's midriff.

The blade sinks deep, parting the creature's skin with minimal resistance. Another screech erupts from its distended mouth, this one loud enough to dislodge small clumps of earth from the tunnel ceiling. The thin blood flows more freely from this new wound, running down the dagger's handle to coat Akantha's fingers in its foul slickness.

She withdraws the blade and steps back, creating distance to reassess. The Fisher Folk clutches at this new injury, its movements becoming less coordinated as fluid leaks from both wounds. Yet it shows no signs of retreating or surrendering.

It lunges again, both arms extended this time, reaching for Akantha's throat with fingers that spread freakishly wide. She ducks beneath the attack leaving the creature's arms passing through empty air where her head had been moments before. Her counter-slash misses as well, the Fisher Folk again proving more agile than its gangly frame suggests.

They evaluate each other in the limited space. The torch in Akantha's left hand throws wild shadows as she keeps it elevated for visibility. The Fisher Folk seems to shy away from the direct light, its oversized eyes blinking rapidly when the flame's illumination hits them directly. It uses the tunnel wall for support, one webbed hand leaving smears of yellowish fluid on the packed earth.

Akantha feints left, drawing the creature's attention before changing direction abruptly. The Fisher Folk falls for the deception, committing to block a attack that never materialises. As it realises its error, she scores another hit, a shallow slash across what might be its ribcage, opening another line of seeping fluid that drips onto the tunnel floor.

The creature howls in frustration and pain, abandoning any pretence of tactical thought. It throws itself forward in a final, desperate attack, both arms swinging wildly. One misses entirely, but the other connects with Akantha's hastily raised buckler. The impact drives her backward a step, her boot slipping slightly on the damp floor.

The torch wobbles dangerously in her grip, the flame guttering as it's jolted by the sudden movement. For one heart-stopping moment, it seems certain to extinguish, plunging them into darkness where the Fisher Folk's adapted eyes would give it an overwhelming advantage. Somehow Akantha maintains her hold, steadying her hand through sheer determination.

The Fisher Folk presses its advantage, sensing her momentary imbalance. It crowds closer, those elongated limbs hemming her in against the tunnel wall, its body hunched forward to bring its needle-toothed mouth within striking distance of her face.

Then, from the shadows behind the creature, Mardonius emerges.

His approach is silent, his footfalls masked by the sounds of the Fisher Folk's laboured breathing and Akantha's struggle. One moment the creature looms over her, the next Mardonius stands behind it, mace already in mid-swing.

The weapon's metal head catches the torchlight as it arcs through the air, momentum building until it connects with the back of the Fisher Folk's elongated skull. The impact produces a sound unlike anything Mardonius has heard in countless battles. There is no crack of breaking bone but something wetter, softer, like a melon dropped onto stone. The creature's head distorts under the force, the thin skull giving way completely as the mace crushes through to the matter beneath.

Death is instantaneous. The Fisher Folk's body goes completely limp, collapsing to the tunnel floor in a tangle of overlong limbs, yellowish fluid starts pooling beneath its ruined head. The stench intensifies briefly before settling into something almost tolerable by comparison, the difference between active decay and the stillness that follows.

Mardonius and Akantha lock eyes across the fallen creature, both breathing heavily, adrenaline still coursing through their systems. No words are necessary. It is a moment of shared respect between warriors who have survived their first battle together.

The silence that follows feels unnatural after the chaos of combat. It is broken only by their laboured breathing and the soft dripping of yellowish fluid onto the mud floor. Akantha lowers her torch slightly, giving her arm relief even as she maintains enough light to survey their surroundings. Her eyes move from the fallen Fisher Folk at her feet to Mardonius, then beyond him to the wider space from which he emerged.

"The other?" she asks, her voice steady despite the exertion of battle. Blood trickles from a small cut on her cheek where something, perhaps a claw or tooth, caught her during the struggle. She makes no move to wipe it away, allowing the crimson line to trace the contour of her face.

Mardonius gestures back toward the chamber behind him. "Female. Unconscious I think, not dead." He regulates his breathing to ensure a clear head and maintain his focus, just as he was trained. "There are younglings too. Infants."

A shadow passes across Akantha's face but it is not compassion, it is something darker and more resolute. "Show me."

She steps over the fallen Fisher Folk without a second glance, her boots leaving prints in the yellowish fluid pooling beneath its shattered skull. The smell clings to everything now. It will stay in their clothes, their hair, their memories long after they leave this place.

Mardonius leads her into the wider chamber, where the female Fisher Folk remains slumped against the wall just as his mace strike had left her. The creature's chest rises and falls in shallow movements, she is unconscious but alive. The misshapen head lolls to one side, yellowish fluid leaking from one ear and the corner of its distended mouth. Its many breasts hang limply against its ribcage, the skin there mottled with patches of darker pigmentation.

Akantha studies the fallen creature for a long moment, her expression unreadable in the flickering torchlight. Then she crosses the muddy floor to stand before it. Her dagger remains in her hand, the blade still coated with the thin blood of the larger one.

"Twisted cannot change," she says, the words carrying the weight of long-held experience. "Born wrong. Die wrong." There is no hesitation in her voice, no questioning of the action she's about to take.

With the same efficiency she might use to dispatch a wounded deer or fox, Akantha places her boot on the female's chest, pinning it against the wall. The creature stirs slightly at the pressure but doesn't fully regain consciousness. Akantha leans forward, driving her dagger into the exposed throat with a single, decisive thrust.

The blade slides in with minimal resistance, parting the pale flesh and severing whatever passes for a windpipe in these creatures. The female's eyes fly open at the mortal wound; bulbous orbs rolling wildly before focusing on Akantha's face. Recognition flashes across those inhuman features, not of Akantha specifically, but of what she represents. Death at human hands.

A gurgling sound emerges from the punctured throat as yellowish fluid fountains around the embedded blade.

Akantha maintains pressure, neither twisting the knife nor withdrawing it until the creature's struggles weaken and cease. Only then does she remove the blade, wiping it clean against the Fisher Folk's own skin before straightening.

A spatter of the thin blood marks her face and neck like pale freckles. She makes no move to clean it, seemingly unbothered by the foul substance. Instead, she spits on the creature's corpse, the gesture carrying such concentrated contempt that Mardonius almost feels it as a physical force. She mutters a curse in her native tongue, bitter words that need no translation given their context.

Her attention shifts to the mud floor, where the two infant Fisher Folk continue their blind wriggling. Their mewling cries have grown more insistent, perhaps sensing their mother's death through whatever primitive connection exists between them. They are pitiful things, malformed parodies of human babies, their limbs already displaying the unnatural elongation that would only grow more pronounced with age.

Mardonius watches Akantha closely, curious how she'll respond to these defenceless creatures. In his experience, even hardened soldiers sometimes hesitate when confronted with enemy young, a natural response that transcends battle training. He feels no particular compassion for these Twisted infants himself, but recognises the moral complexity their existence presents.

Akantha shows no such conflict. Without pause or ceremony, she crouches beside the first infant, her dagger finding its throat with the same lack of hesitation she demonstrated with the mother. The tiny body convulses once, then stills. She moves immediately to the second, repeating the action. Neither kill takes more than seconds to complete.

When she rises, her face remains impassive, betraying neither satisfaction nor regret. She cleans her blade more thoroughly this time, using a relatively clean patch of her tunic to remove the worst of the fluid before returning the weapon to its sheath.

"Twisted breed Twisted," she says simply, meeting Mardonius' gaze directly. "Like rot in fruit. Must cut all away."

Something in her eyes challenges him to disagree, to voice some objection to the clinical elimination of creatures that had no choice in their own existence. But Mardonius offers no criticism. His years patrolling the eastern borders have shown him the consequences of mercy misplaced, the villages razed because a patrol commander couldn't bring themselves to kill something that looked harmless despite its nature.

Instead, he shrugs, acknowledging both her action and its necessity. "We should search this place," he says, returning to their mission's purpose. "The courier and the brass case might be here."

Akantha's posture relaxes slightly, perhaps relieved by his lack of judgment. The torch in her hand sputters, reminding them of their limited time. They have perhaps five minutes of light remaining before darkness claims this underground domain.

"Search quick," she agrees, already moving toward what appears to be a crude sleeping area in one corner of the chamber.

Mardonius cannot help but notice that the same woman who'd barely acknowledged him only an hour ago, now signals with a quick hand gesture when she finds nothing beneath a pile of sticks. He is glad for it. They might not be friends, nor even allies, but they'd survived by working together, and that counted for something.

CHAPTER 9

The hemispherical chamber reeks of death and river muck, a nauseating blend that clings to the back of Mardonius' throat even as he settles his breath. Akantha unconsciously wipes yellowish Fisher Folk blood from her face with the back of her hand, smearing rather than cleaning the foul substance. They know time is running out, both for their makeshift light source and their opportunity to reach Swansbane before nightfall.

"We search quick," Akantha says, her voice tight with urgency. She raises the torch higher, illuminating the crude living space of the Fisher Folk. The curved walls of packed earth rise to form a dome overhead, the surface marked with strange patterns, scratches that might be writing or simply territorial markers. The floor dips toward the soaked centre where a nest of rotting vegetation forms what passes for a bed.

Mardonius is already moving toward the far side of the chamber where the shadows seem deeper. "Check for passages," he instructs, shield still readied despite the apparent death of all immediate threats. The army taught him well that survival depends on thoroughness and that assumptions kill faster than enemies.

Dividing the space between them without the need for discussion, Akantha probes the edges of the chamber with her spear, disturbing piles of unidentifiable detritus. The torch flames shrinks perceptibly, reaching the last layer of its fuel. Its light wavers enough that she has resorted to putting bits of dried material she finds on it in an attempt to extend its life.

"Here," Mardonius calls, his voice low despite the apparent absence of further enemies. His search has uncovered a gap in the chamber wall, a narrow passage barely visible in the diminishing light. "Another tunnel."

Akantha crosses to him, holding the torch forward. The flame illuminates a crawlspace roughly three feet in diameter leading into darkness. The stench that emanates from it is different from the general miasma of the chamber, it is sharper with the unmistakable sweetness of advanced decay.

"Courier might be there," she suggests, her nose wrinkling at the intensified smell.

Mardonius peers into the opening. "I'll go first. Follow with the light."

The passage is mercifully short, no more than six feet in length. The packed earth presses against his shoulders and back, small roots hanging from the ceiling catch in his hair and scrape his scalp. His boots slide through something slick that he chooses not to identify. Behind him, Akantha's breathing sounds unnaturally loud in the confined space, the torch's crackling nearly deafening.

The tunnel opens suddenly into a small chamber, being more of a widened pocket in the earth than a proper room. Mardonius pulls himself forward into the space, his mind registering several details. The chamber is roughly circular, perhaps eight feet across. The ceiling hangs much lower than in the main room, leaving him little headroom. And most importantly, dominating the centre of the floor lies a fetid heap of cloth and bones.

At the top of the heap a human's remains lie in a jumbled pile, as if carelessly tossed aside after being stripped of flesh. The skull rests slightly apart from the main mass, its eye sockets filled with mud and jaw hanging open in a silent scream. What little flesh remains has turned a mottled grey, pulled tight against bone in some places, sagging in bloated pockets in others. The stench is overwhelming, a physical force that makes Mardonius' eyes water despite his experience with battlefields and their aftermath.

Akantha emerges from the tunnel behind him, the torch casting dramatic shadows that make the bones seem to move with ghoulish animation. She gags once before controlling her reaction, her free hand coming up to cover her nose and mouth.

"Eanna's mercy," she mutters.

Mardonius kneels beside the remains, forcing himself to override his natural revulsion. "Help came too late for him," he says quietly. With careful movements, he reaches for the skull, lifting it from the mud with more gentleness than he'd shown the living Fisher Folk. "We'll take this. He deserves a proper burial."

Akantha raises an eyebrow but doesn't question the decision. She understands rituals for the dead, even if their specific forms differ between their cultures.

"It's important," Mardonius adds as an afterthought, meeting her eyes across the flickering torchlight. "No one's spirit should remain in this place."

She says nothing but shifts her stance to maintain watch over the tunnel through which they entered. Her spear remains ready, her body poised to attack despite their apparent solitude. The torch continues its steady decline, the flame now barely stronger than a candle's.

Mardonius sets the skull carefully aside before turning his attention to the remainder of the courier's possessions. He sifts through the pile methodically, separating bone from fabric from personal effects. The dead man's clothing has been largely shredded, but objects tucked within its folds have survived the Fisher Folk's initial plundering.

A large leather bag emerges first, its surface stained dark with river water and worse substances. Inside, cushioned in wadded cloth, he finds a small glass mirror, its surface cracked but still reflective. The firelight catches in its fractured surface, sending tiny shards of brightness dancing across the chamber walls.

Next comes a fishing pole, collapsed into sections and bound with twine. Beside it lies a black stone pendant shaped like a coiled snake, hanging from a leather string gone stiff with dried fluids. Mardonius holds it up briefly before adding it to their growing collection of salvage.

His fingers close around something smooth and geometric; a thumb-sized three-sided prism of translucent orange crystal or glass. He turns it in the torchlight, watching how it captures and transforms the flame's glow. A verdigris-stained copper flute joins the collection, its once-intricate engravings now barely visible beneath the green patina. Mardonius blows gently to clear mud from its holes, incidentally revealing that the instrument remains functionally intact despite its apparent age.

His heart quickens as his fingers brush against a small leather pouch. Coins. He opens it carefully, counting by touch in the dying light: one copper and fourteen brass bits. A modest sum by any standard, yet his pulse jumps at the discovery.

"Found something?" Akantha asks, her posture shifting forward.

"Money," Mardonius confirms, holding up the pouch. "Not much, but better than nothing."

Her eyes lock onto the coins, her hunger for them as plain as if she were staring at a hot meal after days without. The brass catches what little torchlight remains, reflecting in her gaze. The unspoken matter of division looms between them. Her eyes betray the same desperate arithmetic he performs in his own mind, counting out survival one brass bit at a time.

Throughout his search, the stench of decay never diminishes. It coats their skin, infiltrates their clothing, forcing them to breathe through their mouths in shallow gasps. Mardonius finds himself swallowing repeatedly, fighting his body's natural urge to reject the contents of his stomach. Sweat beads on his forehead despite the underground chill, his stomach clenching with the effort of maintaining composure in this charnel pit.

The torch gives a particularly violent sputter, the flame shrinking alarmingly before stabilising at an even smaller size. Their remaining light can now be measured in minutes. Mardonius intensifies his search, hands moving more quickly through the remaining debris, seeking the brass case that represents their primary objective.

Mardonius' fingers close around something cylindrical hidden beneath the courier's tattered clothing, smooth, cool metal that stands out among the organic decay surrounding it. He brushes away clinging mud to reveal a gleaming brass tube about the length of his forearm. The scroll case. Relief floods through him, temporarily overwhelming the stench and exhaustion. Their primary objective, found at last.

"Got it," he announces, lifting the case for Akantha to see. The brass catches the dying torchlight, throwing warm reflections across the cramped chamber.

Akantha's expression shifts from vigilant tension to satisfied relief. "Good. Now we leave." Her eyes flick toward the sputtering torch. "No time."

Mardonius wipes more mud from the case's surface, revealing intricate engravings that spiral around its length. The craftsmanship surpasses anything they have discovered until now, with the tubes' intricate lines creating patterns that could be purely decorative or carry a significance he cannot understand. One end of the tube bears a cap secured with a thick dollop of red wax, pressed with a sigil he doesn't recognise.

"Look," he says, turning the seal toward Akantha. "Know this mark?"

She leans closer, squinting in the dimming light. The wax shows what might be a stylised fountain surrounded by a circle of small symbols.

"No," she admits after a moment. "Not Takaz'Ran. Not Randeri." Her finger hovers over the wax without touching it. "Old, maybe."

Mardonius attempts to twist the cap, testing whether it might open without disturbing the seal. It remains firmly in place, the wax bond unbroken despite whatever rough handling the Fisher Folk might have given it. The case's contents remain as securely sealed as the day the courier departed with them.

"Can't open it without breaking seal," he concludes, setting the case carefully aside with their other salvage. "Not our business anyway."

His attention returns to the coin pouch. He upends it into his hand, the metal pieces clinking softly against each other. One copper coin, worth ten brass bits on its own, and fourteen brass bits, spread before them like a king's ransom. In his years as a soldier he might have spent this much on a single night's drinking. Now, it represents a significant haul.

Without discussion, he divides the pile into two equal shares; the twelve brass bits for himself, the copper and two bits for Akantha.

"Yours," he says simply, watching as she quickly tucks the coins into the coin pouch at her belt. "Equal danger, equal effort, equal pay. We are in this together."

Her eyes gleam with poorly concealed satisfaction. "Good pay. Better than expected."

"Better than nothing," he corrects, but he can't suppress the similar satisfaction warming his chest. Just half of those brass bits would buy a poor but filling meal at most inns. Added to his existing funds means he's marginally closer to affording the seven silvers for the spear he has come to realise he needs.

The torch gives another violent sputter, the flame shrinking to little more than a glowing ember. Darkness presses in around them like a physical presence, the air suddenly seeming thicker and even harder to breathe.

"Time to go," Mardonius says, gathering their findings quickly.

He wraps the skull in a salvaged piece of cloth, tucking it carefully into his pack. The mirror, pendant, prism, and flute join it, each item potentially valuable to the right buyer. The fishing pole he holds alongside his shield. Most importantly, he secures the brass case within an inner flap of his leather armour, where it presses comfortingly against his ribs.

Akantha backs toward the tunnel entrance, maintaining her watch position even as she prepares to retreat. "You first," she directs, holding the torch to provide what little illumination remains for his passage.

He emerges into the main chamber immediately taking a defensive stance out of habit. The bodies of the Fisher Folk lie where they fell, beginning to stiffen as death tightens its grip. The infants' tiny corpses seem smaller now, shrivelling in their own end. Mardonius steps carefully around them, refusing to acknowledge the uncomfortable weight in his chest at the sight.

Akantha follows, emerging from the tunnel with the nearly dead torch held high. Its light barely reaches two feet now and the darkness beyond seems all the more impenetrable by contrast. They cross the main chamber quickly, neither of them speaking nor looking at the carnage they've left behind. The mud sucks at their boots with each step, as if the very ground tries to hold them back.

The return tunnel stretches before them, its dimensions unchanged yet somehow less threatening than before. Mardonius takes the lead again, shield forward, every sense strained for any indication of danger. The packed earth walls feel wider now, the ceiling higher, though logic tells him nothing has physically changed.

"Torch won't last," Akantha warns from behind him, her voice tight with urgency.

Mardonius increases his pace, navigating the bends and narrowings from memory now as much as sight. The brass case presses against his ribs with each movement, a constant reminder of their successfully completed mission. They've found what they came for. All that remains is escape.

The tunnel curves ever so slightly upward, angling toward the distant surface. Mardonius' legs burn with the effort of the climb, muscles protesting after the exertion of combat followed by the awkward crouching and crawling the muddy floor requires. Behind him, Akantha's breathing grows more laboured, though she offers no complaint.

The torch gives one final, desperate flare, a momentary brightening that illuminates the tunnel walls with surprising clarity, before guttering out completely. Darkness swallows them whole, absolute and oppressive.

"Keep moving," Mardonius says into the blackness. "Follow the slope up."

They proceed by touch alone, one hand on the wall, the other extended forward or backward to maintain contact with each other. The darkness is disorienting, stripping away distance and direction until only the upward slope provides guidance. Mardonius feels sweat beading on his forehead despite the cool underground air, his heart hammering against his ribs.

After what feels like hours, even though it could only be minutes, the glow from the sun outside this infernal tunnel begins to flow into the space. Finally, thankfully, they'd reached the junction where their path meets the rope leading to the surface. Through the opening above, noontime daylight filters down. It is painfully bright after the absolute darkness of the tunnel, yet the most welcome sight Mardonius has beheld in recent memory.

The rope hangs where they left it, a lifeline to the world above. Mardonius grasps it, testing the knots with a sharp tug before turning to the darkness where Akantha must be.

"We made it," he says, relief evident in his voice despite all former attempts at professional detachment. "Rope's still secure. I'll go first, make sure it's safe up there."

"Quickly," she responds from somewhere close beside him. "We must be soon on road."

Mardonius grips the rope firmly, preparing to haul himself upward toward daylight and fresh air. The brass case shifts against his ribs, its weight a comfort rather than a burden. Mission accomplished, or at least the first part. Now they need only reach Swansbane before whatever horrors that supposedly prowl the night can find them. He begins haul himself upwards, muscles protesting but spirit lifting with each inch closer to the surface, leaving the Fisher Folk lair behind, at least in body, if not in memory.

CHAPTER 10

Mardonius pulls himself from the dark wound in the earth, each inch up the rope an age. Then the rush: light, air, sky. He lies gasping like a fish on the bank of a strange river. Fresh air fills his lungs. Akantha climbs out after him, then kneels on the damp sunlit soil gathering her breath. They don't pause long to recover; the sun has not moved as far as they fear, but they remember Lukkar's warning.

Up near the road they dig a quick pit in drier ground. Mardonius respectfully places the skull within, it looks unsettlingly small.

Together they replace the dirt, pat it down and set stones as a crude marker. "The view for his spirit is clean here," Akantha states looking down towards the river.

"It is a far cleaner place to lie than in that pit." replies Mardonius.

The road and sunset call to them and this time they listen. They grab their gear, stash their findings in backpack and bag and trade the light of weak torch for the dappled sunshine pouring through a forest that seems a little less fearful now.

Mardonius peels off the ring mail, each metal circle catching the light as he carefully folds it in its protective cloth and places it into his pack. Akantha leans forward on her donkey, eyes narrowing with curiosity.

"Why wear metal that slows?" she asks out of genuine interest.

"I could buy an acre of good farmland with the money this costs," he answers, patting the wrapped armour, "But, years of watching men die taught me to trade speed for survival." He pauses and looks down the road, "And speaking of speed, and survival..."

The road stretches west, haunting in its remoteness. Its paved surface was once white and grand but now dirt and moss cover its proud construction, a skin laid by many centuries of neglect. Once, it bore the weight of caravans and was perhaps marched upon by the armies of the Empire of Chilissar in military precision. Now it holds only two travellers and the scattered bones of an slaughtered horse.

They set off. Mardonius immediately falls into the steady march stride of the Legion. This time Akantha rides a donkey's length ahead. She doesn't look back. He closes the gap, admitting only to himself the envy he feels for the way she rides. His childhood taught him tracking, woodcraft, silence, but never riding. His military years taught him pain, discipline and even more silence, but never riding. Mass combat taught him that the greatest fear of any foot soldier is the enemy cavalry. Now he is not sure which he fears the most; horses or boats.

It is said that the Takaz'Ran are a people who learn to ride before they can walk. Watching Akantha's straight back and settled posture he can believe that.

The afternoon eases towards dusk. The sun's last bold
efforts catching Akantha's form in silhouette as she rides
ahead. Mardonius' stride shortens to adjust to the
growing slope they are now on, the road has been
climbing for a while now and this last section is steep.
Each step feels like effort now, exhaustion from their
fight with the Fisher Folk and the brutal pace he kept
spreading a soreness over his body. The shadows stretch
behind them appear to double the space they've covered.
Still, Akantha sits straight-backed, though even she
must feel the ache of her wounds. He can see a livid
bruise on her arm but she has said nothing of it. They
progress in silence, though this silence lacks the
awkwardness of this morning.

Wooded land surrounds them, the expanse is bleak and
unfamiliar. The weight of travel presses heavy on
Mardonius. His mind retraces the steps they've taken:
up from the river, through deep forest and now forested
hills. For the longest time the Upper Gift River mirrored
their path but now even that is gone, swallowed up
behind the hills they climb. As much as they are sore and
tired the end of this leg of their journey is near. They
know that at the top of this incline lies Swansbane.

They say little, Mardonius at least saves his breath for
the climb. The only sound is the persistent crunch of his
footfalls and of the donkey's plodding hooves. Akantha
occasionally turns her head, an almost imperceptible
glance, as if to reassure herself that he is still keeping up.

The road twists now, winding upwards toward the
settlement Lukkar refused to speak of.

Each step is an effort, soreness spreading and reminding Mardonius of the long hours spent fighting, marching, surviving.

The hill's crest finally appears. From this vantage point, the town stretches before them, perched defiantly at the very top of this hill. His breath escapes in a gust, relief washing over him with realisation. They've reached Swansbane. It is still daylight.

The forest that hugged the road has been cut back here, creating an open wound of cleared land in front of the settlement. The emptiness seems to be more than just overharvesting, there is intention here. It begins at Swansbane's walls and extends outwardly before ending abruptly perhaps 300 paces hence.

The entire town clings to the edge of a sheer cliff, looking for all the world like an army holding position with nothing at its back. The weakening rays of the sun's light catch the walls and buildings, tracing their outlines before losing itself in the canyon far below. What lies behind this cliff must be the remains of the Upper Gift River.

The open space that fronts the town shows signs of cultivation. Patches of carefully tended soil promise crops as well as being poor cover for any who thought to approach. Mardonius lets his attention travel the length of the cleared land then back to the settlement.

They have reached the town with time to spare, nearly an hour's sun remaining. Relief overtakes weariness in his bones. However, the satisfaction is tempered by great surprise at what he sees. This is no simple trading outpost. This is a fortress.

A soldier's eye can read the landscape like a map. It sees what must be seen for survival's sake. Swansbane's defences leap out at Mardonius, this is a town built for siege. A thick log wall encircles the town and that wall has interspersed stone-reinforcement within it to bear the weight of assault. The walls themselves are immense, shored with the precision of skilled builders. This is no ragtag militia's hurried fortifications; these are defences worthy of a place constantly under threat. It is a stark testament to endurance, a statement that will echo long after the need has passed. The logs are thick. Cut and fitted with expert care. Each piece of stone placed to ensure every hand's width is designed for survival.

Mardonius scans the outer perimeter, noting a ring of sharpened stakes. They jut outward at aggressive and unpredictable angles, ready to skewer those who rush the first line. His mind fills the gaps with imagined bodies, enemies pinned and twitching. The open space itself serves as more than just farmland, it becomes a killing field for the defenders. Archers could pick off invaders with ease.

Even watching the distant figures move along the parapets confirms his impression. Training. Readying. Watching. He knows their type well.

This is not the kind of village he'd expect to find at the end of a lonely road, just a day's travel from a friendly neighbouring town. He finds himself stop, in a rare lapse of composure, to just stare with a mixture of amazement and unease.

The extent of the preparations tells a story, one of isolation, of determination certainly, but more importantly, of an ever-present enemy. No trading outpost needs to maintain this level of alertness unless it expects assault.

No, he corrected himself, unless it expects regular assault.

For these defences to be necessary, for such careful measures to exist in what should be the hinterlands, Swansbane must be at war. Constantly and against the strongest foes. His mind races to grasp it: what terrible enemy attacks here? Theories form and shatter like ice beneath a sudden thaw. It truly makes no sense.

Akantha patiently waits for him to catch up. Her face is set with the same fierce concentration he saw during their fight, but now there's something else. A question in her eyes. She lets nothing out, instead patiently allowing him close the distance. He certainly doesn't trust himself to voice his thoughts.

"Smell that?" she says, looking to the sky instead of his face.

He pauses, sifting the air. There, beneath the earthy scent of tilled soil and the rich, damp tang of the nearby woods. Faint but unmistakable. The oily, smoky trace of burned flesh. Confirmation of his worst fears, the only missing piece to this grim tableau.

They resume their approach. The closer they get, the more impressive the defences appear. Mardonius feels the prickling unease of a soldier who knows he is approaching the front line but is yet to see the enemy.

Swansbane swallows them whole as they draw closer. Even at distance, the massive gates in the wall feel imposing. They are more like what one would find in a castle than a settlement. The size of the doors alone suggests the handiwork of Dwarves. They have strong beams and thick bands of metal that speak of intense preparation. The gates are an edifice unto themselves, capable of standing as separate monuments. Mardonius imagines them closing, barring entry to the night and its terrors. The thickness, the cross-beams, the riveted joints, each stronger and far heavier than any trading post requires. He can picture the mechanism that would be needed to secure them, the deep thunk of massive bolts sliding home.

Figures in brown, grey, and green trudge toward these open gates. They are burdened with planks and pelts, their heads lowered in determination. Each person is armed, even the children openly carry long thrusting daggers. Humans and a group of Dwarves walk together without pause. It is the kind of unity Mardonius has seen only in war.

He walks the last stretch toward the town in stunned silence, taking in the details that transform this place from myth to reality. Mardonius sees it all with a soldier's perspective, assessing the strength, the intent, the underlying determination that must drive such construction.

The figures approaching the gates come into sharper focus, shedding their anonymity as they near. Some carry hunting spoils, others bundles of rough-hewn timber. Furs and skins suggest successful forays into the surrounding wilds. A handful of workers show the unmistakable marks of miners, their faces streaked with dirt that looks like war paint, their bodies laden with gear that clinks like weaponry. Mardonius notes that even these are armed, in jarring contrast to most labourers he's encountered in towns throughout Rande. The weapons vary, some mass-produced and basic, others finely wrought, but all capable of defence or offence.

He looks to Akantha, wondering if she sees the same patterns, the same desperate practicality disguised as ordinary life. Her expression remains unreadable, but he knows she must recognise the signs. A people ready. A people never at rest.

As the details sharpen, he spots younger faces among the adults. Older children and teenagers who, in other places, might show smiles, curiosity or youthful disdain. Here, they wear the same severe expressions as the grown men and women. They appear just as well armed and just as determined.

Mardonius scans for the usual distinctions, for the separations that mark people by sex, role or rank. Instead, he finds the opposite. There appears to be a lack of hierarchy, a cohesion that ignores the divisions that make up regular society.

It is the Humans and Dwarves moving together with obvious unity that is more striking to him than any other visible differences. Ever since the war with the Brotherhood of Tszzarb, a nation whose 'brotherhood' is between Humans and Dwarves, a Dwarf was seen only as a necessary evil in Rande. Their knowledge, especially with mining, forging and jewellery, being seen as barely adequate compensation for the threat they represent.

Still, Swansbane sprawls before them, its construction a testament to function over form. Wooden buildings dominate the town, interspersed with patches of finely dressed marble and stone that suggest scavenging from ruins rather than fresh quarrying. The style is simple, direct, and as utilitarian as the people who inhabit it.

Despite the seeming lack of ornamentation, the town bears signs of prosperity. There is the sheer volume of construction, the raw materials evident in every building, the sense that this place grows rather than dwindles. Mardonius estimates at least 600 inhabitants, it is not small despite its isolation.

At Swansbane's highest point stands a massive structure, its lines are precise, its stonework dressed with uncommon skill. It towers over all else, not merely by height but by presence. He recognised the architectural style immediately – a Temple of Eanna. Its grandeur contrasts starkly with the rest of the settlement. The temple's prominence strikes him as more than just religious dedication. It's the focal point of the town, the hub around which all other activity orbits. To build something so lavish in a place that requires such expensive defensive structures implies an almost fanatical devotion.

Mardonius absorbs it all, the pieces slowly forming a picture that intrigues and unsettles him. Swansbane, with its sprawling construction, its martial readiness, its religious fervour, challenges his every expectation. For a man used to predicting outcomes, it's a place that holds the greatest threat of all. The unexpected.

CHAPTER 11

The Community Hall's thick wooden beams absorb the noise of conversation, reducing dozens of voices to a muted hum that hangs in the air like wood smoke. Mardonius cradles a clay bowl between calloused hands, letting the steam from the venison stew warm his face. Across the rough-hewn table, Akantha mirrors his posture, her shoulders slightly hunched from the day's exertions, her expression guarded but no longer hostile at least.

"Eat," Lukkar urges, pushing a wooden platter of dark bread toward them. "Town baker uses mountain rye. Good for the blood."

The stew's rich aroma fills Mardonius' nostrils, apart from the venison there are root vegetables and herbs he can't immediately identify. His initial spoonful confirms its quality, the meat tender and the broth thick with rendered fat. After a day of hard travel and harder combat, his body craves the sustenance with an urgency that borders on desperation.

Lukkar watches them eat with undisguised amusement, his earlier road-weary persona shed like unnecessary clothing. He sits straighter, speaks clearer, his eyes more alert than they'd appeared during their journey. The transformation isn't total, he still wears the same stained tunic, but the difference is noticeable enough that Mardonius wonders who the real Lukkar is.

"Got something better than water to wash it down," Lukkar announces, gesturing toward a serving girl who hovers near the central hearth. "Three mugs of the dark", he asks of her.

The girl gives nothing back, no flirt, no smile, she just disappears through a side door.

The hall itself feels similar to countless taverns Mardonius has visited, yet fundamentally different in ways he struggles to articulate. Perhaps it's the absence of raucous laughter, or the distance between tables to allow unobstructed movement. Most taverns crams in as many tables as possible, all the better to increase profits and hamper brawls. The patrons here are all heavily armed, some are armoured, but no tension appears to exist among them.

"Dwarven Ale?" Akantha asks, surprise evident in her voice. She sets down her spoon, giving Lukkar her full attention for perhaps the first time. "From Tszzarb?"

"The very same," Lukkar confirms, a small smile playing at the corners of his mouth.

Mardonius tries to hide his own surprise. Dwarven Ale is legendary for its potency and flavour, but more importantly, it's nearly impossible to obtain outside direct trade with Tszzarb. For Swansbane to have it suggests connections that a remote, fortified village shouldn't possess.

"Expensive," Mardonius observes carefully. "And rare."

Lukkar's smile widens. "Not as rare, nor as expensive here as you might think."

Before Mardonius can question this further, the serving girl returns carrying three heavy clay mugs. The liquid within is nearly black, topped with a finger of tan foam that releases a bitter-sweet aroma complex enough to make his mouth water. She carefully places them on the table, spilling not a drop despite the mugs' obvious weight.

"To survival," Lukkar toasts, raising his mug. "Yours today, ours every day."

The ale tastes nothing like the thin, sour brews common to roadside inns. This is deep and complex with bitter herbs balanced against sweet malt, and an earthy undertone that reminds Mardonius of fresh-turned soil. The strength is immediately apparent; warmth spreads from his stomach outward, a pleasant heat that dulls the day's accumulated aches.

"Good?" Lukkar asks, wiping foam from his upper lip.

"Why didn't you tell us more about this place?" Mardonius counters, unwilling to be distracted by hospitality, however genuine. "You were obviously being vague about Swansbane."

Lukkar shrugs, the gesture almost apologetic. "Words don't capture this place right." He looks around the hall, his expression growing distant. "You had to see it. Experience it. Otherwise, you'd think I was spinning tales or gone mad."

Mardonius slowly scans the room, taking in details he missed initially. The hall's patrons eat as through it is a job, their conversations brief and purposeful. No one lingers over empty plates. No one drinks to excess. Even laughter, when it occurs, feels muted and contained, as if permitted rather than spontaneous.

"We explored the town earlier," Akantha says, her words carefully neutral. She tears a piece of bread, using it to wipe the last traces of stew from her bowl. "Different from other towns."

Lukkar snorts. "Different. That's one way to put it." He leans forward, voice dropping. "You noticed, I'm sure. No playing children. No idle chatter. Everyone with purpose. Everyone with weapons." He taps the table with a calloused finger. "Everyone ready."

"Ready for what?" Mardonius asks, though he already suspects the answer.

"Night," Lukkar responds simply. "And what comes with it."

Mardonius remembers their walk through Swansbane's streets just hours ago. The eerie quiet, the focussed movement of its inhabitants, the weapons carried openly by everyone from gray-haired elders to solemn-faced children. The entire settlement operates more like a military camp than village, preparing for an assault from an enemy he can't begin to guess at.

"How long has it been like this?"

"Longer than anyone knows," Lukkar says. He drains half his mug in a single swallow, then wipes his mouth with the back of his hand. "Some say since the founding. Some say it was different once, centuries back." His eyes meet Mardonius' directly. "Does it matter? This is what survival looks like here."

Akantha shifts beside him, her posture subtly changing. He recognises the adjustment. She redistributes her weight for quicker movement, straightening her spine to improve her awareness of surroundings. He's making the same unconscious changes. Something about this place awakens the warrior instincts, even in the relative safety of a communal meal.

"You delivered the wagon?" Mardonius asks, choosing to steer the conversation toward mundane matters. "Master Gynn's goods?"

"Delivered and received," Lukkar confirms. "They're already unloading. Efficiency is religion here, second only to actual religion of course." He glances toward the ceiling, in the general direction of the temple they'd visited earlier. "And even that serves a purpose beyond faith."

A bell sounds somewhere in the distance. It is no alarm, but is instead a signal toll to communicate some regular event. Throughout the hall, heads lift in unison, attention captured by the sound. Several patrons rise immediately, collecting weapons leaned against tables or nearby walls before filing out in wordless coordination.

"Watch change," Lukkar explains, noting their observation. "Four-hour shifts on the wall, day and night." He gestures toward the bowls before them. "Finish up. Night's young yet, but rest comes at a premium here."

Mardonius takes another pull of the ale, savouring its complexity while watching the silent choreography of Swansbane's residents. His training recognises the pattern; the discipline, the readiness, the unspoken communication that comes from shared purpose under constant threat. These are not merchants, farmers or craftspeople, despite their occupations. These are soldiers who happen to perform other functions between battles.

The ale's warmth radiates through his chest, yet fails to thaw the ice that formed when he first glimpsed Swansbane's fortifications. Tomorrow's he and Akantha will put this place behind them, bearing its uncovered secrets back to Aissentur's comparative sanctuary. Tonight, however, they must find rest within these besieged walls, walls that have stood vigilant against some nameless threat since before anyone can remember.

Earlier that day, they were able to use what was left of the sun to follow a stone-faced stable hand to a long, low building near the eastern gate. The stables smelled of clean hay rather than the expected reek of manure, there appeared to be few beasts in town. Mardonius watched as Akantha fussed over her donkey, checking the donkey's hooves and brushing road dust from its coat with methodical care. She'd spoken softly in her native tongue, the words incomprehensible but the sentiment clear, reassurance, and gratitude for faithful service.

"Animal is important to you," Mardonius stated as he passing her a small cloth bag of feed they'd purchased at the gate.

Akantha had accepted the bag without taking her eyes off her mount. "Ferzif'Eanna carried me from Takaz'Ran land. Knows the way back." Her hands moved with quick precision over the donkey's flanks. "One day, she will be companion to my war horse."

The stable hand had waited with statue-like patience, showing neither boredom nor impatience as they tended to the animal. When they finished, he'd simply pointed toward the main thoroughfare. "Town centre that way. Temple at the top. Market below."

They'd emerged into the last rays of the sun which barely managed to peek around the bigger and higher buildings in the middle of the village. Streets radiated outward from the central hill like spokes from a wheel hub, each packed-earth lane wide enough for wagons but currently carrying only pedestrians.

"Where now?" Mardonius questioned.

Akantha had patted the bag where they'd stored their findings from the Fisher Folk lair. "Somewhere to sell these."

They'd wandered downhill first, drawn by the rhythmic clanging of metal on metal, the smithies occupied a long row of open-fronted buildings. Smoke rose from conical chimneys that vented forge heat skyward. Unlike in other towns, where each smith worked in jealous isolation, these forges appeared to operate in concert. Mardonius counted seven separate work stations, each with their own frontage to the street, yet they functioned with the coordination of a single organism.

A grey-haired woman with arms corded like oak roots pumped massive bellows at the central forge, maintaining the perfect heat while two men, one young, one middle-aged, took turns drawing red-hot metal from the coals. A third man, his face a map of burn scars, hammered the heated metal with metronomic precision. To their left, a similarly coordinated team shaped smaller pieces, arrowheads from the look of them, dozens falling into water barrels with a constant hiss of steam.

"No competition," Mardonius had murmured, noting how each smith anticipated the others' needs without verbal communication. "No individual pride."

"Survival has no room for pride," Akantha had replied, her eyes tracking the movement of tools from hand to hand.

Adjacent to the smithies, they'd found the fletchers' workshop. It was a long hall where wan sunlight poured through high windows onto rows of women and children working at low tables. Their fingers moved with hypnotic rhythm, cutting feathers and binding them to arrow shafts with thin strips of sinew. Even the youngest workers, some no more than six or seven years old, maintained solemn focus on their tasks. No games, no laughter, no childish distractions from work that directly contributed to the town's defence.

A bald man with one milky eye oversaw the operation, moving between tables to inspect completed arrows. When he spoke, his voice never rose above a murmur, yet the workers responded instantly to his corrections. Mardonius recognised the dynamics immediately, no civilian workshop this. This was a production line, where every individual understood their role in a greater purpose.

"They make enough arrows for an army," he'd observed as they moved past. "Thousand per week, at that production rate."

"But no army come to collect them," Akantha had added, completing the thought that troubled him. "These are for own use."

They'd continued through the town, past woodworkers carving bow staves from fine-grained timber, past leatherworkers crafting armour panels with identical stitching patterns, past provisioners smoking meat in quantities that suggested stockpiling rather than immediate need. Everywhere, the same synchronised productivity, the same absence of idle chatter, the same underlying purpose that united old and young, male and female, Human and Dwarf.

"This is a town preparing for siege," Mardonius had said finally, voicing the conclusion that had been forming since they first glimpsed Swansbane's walls. "But from what enemy? We've seen no sign of warfare, no troop movements in the countryside."

Akantha had offered no answer, her attention drawn to a small shop near the market square. Its wooden sign bore no words, only the painted image of a gemstone. "There," she'd said. "For prism."

The jeweller's shop stood apart from the utilitarian structures surrounding it, its interior well-lit by crystal-clear windows and hanging oil lamps. Behind a polished counter, a woman with intricate silver braids worked a magnifying lens mounted on a jointed brass arm. She'd looked up at their entrance, her face lined with age but her eyes sharp and evaluating.

"Travellers," she'd said, the word neither welcome nor rejection. "What do you need?"

Mardonius had reached into their bag, extracting the orange prism they'd recovered from the Fisher Folk lair. The gem caught the lamplight as he placed it on the counter, its facets throwing tiny rainbows across the polished wood.

The jeweller had picked it up with delicate fingers, examining it through her magnifying lens. "Tourmaline," she'd pronounced after a moment. "Decent size. Good enough clarity. Unusual colour saturation." Her assessment complete, she'd looked up at them. "Four silver coins."

The offer had stunned Mardonius into momentary silence. The amount exceeded his expectations tenfold. From Akantha's sharp intake of breath, he knew she felt similar surprise.

"Acceptable," he'd managed, trying to wind back his reaction.

The transaction completed, they'd stepped back into sunlight with heavier coin pouches – two silver pieces each after splitting the proceeds. Akantha had weighed the coins in her palm, her expression somewhere between satisfaction and resignation.

"How much for your war horse?" Mardonius had asked, remembering her earlier comment.

"Poor quality, twenty silver," she'd replied, closing her fingers around her coins. "Good horse, hundred or more." Her sigh carried the weight of deferred dreams. "Long way to go."

They'd found a general trader next, a cramped shop packed with utilitarian goods rather than luxuries. The owner, a hunched man with arthritis in some fingers, had examined their remaining finds dispassionately.

"Mirror: cracked but usable. Fishing pole: common reed, decent construction. Flute: old, corroded, can clean up." He'd pushed two copper coins across the counter. "Fair value."

Another copper coin each, less impressive than the silver, but welcome nonetheless. Mardonius had noted how Akantha carefully separated the coins in her pouch, perhaps mentally allocating them to different necessities.

As they'd left the trader's shop, the bells had tolled the time, and they'd watched another shift change flow through the streets. Guards descended from the walls to be replaced by fresh sentries, workshops emptying as the evening sucked away the last of the light from the sky. The town maintained its rhythm like a heartbeat, constant and necessary for survival.

"No wasted movement," Mardonius had observed. "No wasted resources." He'd turned to Akantha, finding her already watching him with that inscrutable expression. "This isn't normal."

"Normal depends on what you face," she'd replied simply. "We should see temple. Before too dark."

And so they'd turned uphill, toward the ancient stone structure that dominated Swansbane's skyline, unaware that its mysteries would prove even stranger than the militarised town it looked over.

The path to the temple wound upward in a spiral that granted increasingly panoramic views of Swansbane with each turning. Mardonius had noted how the town's organisation became apparent from this height. There were concentric rings of buildings radiating outward from the central hill, interconnected by straight roads that allowed for rapid movement between any two points. It was, unsurprisingly, a defensive layout, optimised for quick reinforcement of any sector under threat. At the summit, the temple had loomed before them, its weathered columns rising from a platform of stone so ancient that any quarry marks had long since surrendered to time.

"Old," Akantha had observed, running her fingers along a column's fluted surface. "Much older than town."

Mardonius agreed, recognising construction techniques that predated modern methods by centuries. The massive stone blocks of the foundation fit together without mortar, their edges worn smooth by countless seasons of wind and rain. Above them rose columns carved with intricate symbols, not the clean lines of Eanna's star that adorned temples in Rande, but flowing patterns that resembled water streams flowing and merging in an intricate embrace. They looked as though they were being born from and returning to seed pods.

The temple's pediment also depicted scenes Mardonius couldn't immediately interpret. There were figures with arms upraised toward stylised waves, others kneeling before what appeared to be downward facing plants. All were rendered in a style both primitive and sophisticated, the figures elongated beyond natural proportion yet containing a fluid grace that suggested movement frozen in stone.

"Not like Eanna temples in Rande," he'd said, searching for familiar iconography and finding none.

"Temples change with land," Akantha had replied, still focussed on following the carvings upward. "Gods wear different face in different place."

They'd ascended wide steps worn concave by countless feet, passed between columns into a space where the very last light filtered through high narrow windows. The interior stretched longer than expected, its central aisle leading toward a circular chamber ahead. The air inside carried the scent of incense along with a sense of dampness and of something green and growing. It felt very disconcerting in a stone structure.

From the circular chamber had come rhythmic sounds; a rattle keeping steady time, accompanied by soft footfalls. Mardonius and Akantha approached cautiously, stopping at the threshold to observe without interrupting.

In the chamber's centre, a silver bowl the size of a wash basin sat atop a stone pedestal. Water filled it to the brim, its surface occasionally disturbed by droplets falling from an opening in the roof directly above. Around this central feature, a woman in flowing blue robes moved in meditative steps, her body bending and rising like a reed in changing currents. Her dance traced patterns on the floor, concentric circles that spiralled inward toward the water basin, then outward again in unending cycles.

A young man sat cross-legged by the wall, keeping the rhythm steady with a rattle made from dried seeds wrapped in sinew. His attention was fixed on the dancer, his beat flawlessly aligning with her movements, even when she unexpectedly altered her sacred dance. Both performers carried on with their ritual, seemingly unaware of the visitors.

Mardonius' attention had been drawn beyond the dancers to the statue that dominated the chamber's far wall. Unlike any depiction of Eanna he'd encountered before, this figure bore little resemblance to the warrior-judge revered throughout Rande. Instead of armour, she wore robes that flowed like water around her form. Instead of scales and sword, both hands cradled a vessel shaped unmistakably like a womb, from which water eternally poured into a basin at her feet. Her face bore the serene expression of abundant fertility rather than stern judgment, her eyes half-closed in what might be ecstasy or deep contemplation. Around her head, stars formed a crown, the only familiar element connecting this figure to the Eanna of Mardonius' experience.

"That's not..." he'd begun, then stopped, aware that challenging local religious interpretations rarely ended well.

"Not what you know," Akantha had finished for him, her voice neutral. "Same goddess. Different aspect."

The dance had continued for several minutes more before concluding with a final, complex sequence that brought the priestess to her knees before the statue, arms extended in supplication or offering. The rattle had fallen silent, and only the soft plink of water droplets falling into the silver bowl disturbed the silence.

Then the priestess rose and without a word walked off to some sanctum with the young priest in tow.

Akantha had shown little interest in the religious aspects, her attention instead drawn to the carved stone walls. She'd moved along the perimeter, examining markings that appeared to be maps or diagrams, flowing lines that might represent waterways, interspersed with symbols Mardonius couldn't interpret.

They'd eventually left the temple without learning much beyond what observation provided. Something about the priestess's serene certainty had discouraged questions, and Mardonius had felt an uncharacteristic reluctance to probe deeper into Swansbane's faith. Some mysteries, his instincts suggested, were better left unexplored by outsiders.

Their descent from the temple had offered new perspectives on Swansbane's antiquity. From above, the patterns of older foundations became visible beneath newer construction; concentric rings of weathered stone predating the current wooden structures by centuries. In places, ancient walls protruded through the ground like bones breaking through skin, their purpose long forgotten but their presence impossible to ignore, now they were mostly used to anchor some of the larger building's walls.

"How old is this settlement?" Mardonius mused aloud as they followed the spiral path downward. "Those foundations aren't from any recent century."

Akantha had shrugged, her interest in architecture apparently limited. "Old settlements build on older ones. Rivers attract people, across time."

At the southern edge of town, the cliff dropped away into a vast chasm where the Upper Gift River was likely to flow. Here they'd discovered the rusting remains of crane mechanisms. The massive iron constructions stood like skeletal sentinels along the precipice, their once-powerful brackets now empty with no wooden arms to extend over the void below.

"For lowering goods to the river, perhaps?" Mardonius had surmised, leaning cautiously over the edge to glimpse what might remain below. The drop had been dizzying, the canyon floor obscured by distance, mist and shadow. "Or maybe raising them from ships? There must have been a quay down there once."

A passing townsman had noticed their interest, his weathered face tightening with something like concern. He'd adjusted his course to intercept them. "Nothing down there now," he'd said, his tone making it clear the matter wasn't open for discussion. "Best stay back from the edge."

The interaction had reinforced their growing sense that certain questions about Swansbane would not be welcomed. Since then, they'd been more careful about their observations, maintaining the appearance of ordinary travellers rather than curious investigators.

"They're hiding something," Mardonius had said once they were alone again, walking torch-lit lower streets toward the Community Hall.

"Everyone hides something," Akantha had replied, her eyes tracking the movements of townspeople preparing for evening. "Question is. Do their secrets threaten us."

Mardonius had no answer for that.

As night finally claimed Swansbane, they'd watched the finished work shift flow through the town. Torches made from thick pitch were lit at regular intervals along the parapet. Yet again there were no commands nor were there comradely calls at the end of a day's work. The inhabitants remained as stoic and focussed as they had been at work.

There was a clear sense through, that whatever Swansbane feared, it came with darkness. And with that was the knowledge that they would spend at least one night within its walls before departing.

The Community Hall empties gradually as the evening deepens, workers drifting out in small groups, their voices hushed as if conserving energy for more important purposes. Mardonius sits with his back to the wall, watching the room thin while nursing the last of his Dwarven Ale. The warmth it provides feels incomplete now, unable to fully dull the questions arising from their exploration of Swansbane's mysteries. Across the table, Akantha shifts uncomfortably, her right hand unconsciously rising to massage her left upper arm where the Fisher Folk's blow left an angry purple bruise.

"Let me see that," Mardonius says, setting down his empty mug. His voice comes out gruffer than intended, a soldier's command rather than an offer of assistance.

Akantha's eyes narrow, her instinctive resistance to displaying vulnerability to strangers warring with actual need. After a moment's hesitation, she extends her arm across the table, rolling up her tunic's sleeve to expose the injury. The bruise spreads like spilled ink beneath her skin, darkest at the centre where impact met flesh, fading to yellow-green at its edges.

"Looks worse than it is," she says, the familiar dismissal of warriors unwilling to acknowledge pain.

Mardonius recognises the lie but accepts it as necessary. He reaches for his pack, extracting a small leather pouch tied with sinew. Inside lie the components of a field healing kit: clean bandages and a small pot of rendered animal fat infused with medicinal plants among other things. The familiar routine of preparation settles his mind as he prepares his treatment with experienced hands.

"Done this before?" Lukkar asks, watching Mardonius at work.

"Standard for anyone who's seen combat," Mardonius replies, deliberately vague. He warms the fat mixture between his palms to soften it before turning back to Akantha. "This will help with swelling."

Her arm remains extended, a gesture of trust that feels more significant than the words they've exchanged. Mardonius applies the poultice with careful pressure, his fingertips working the medicine into skin with movements learned through years of treating fallen comrades. Akantha's muscles tense initially, then gradually relax under his ministrations.

"Good?" he asks, focusing his full attention on the bruise.

"Good." she replies as he wraps a bandage around her arm to keep the poultice in place

Once done she tests his work with small movements of her arm. "Strong herbs," she comments, sniffing at the mixture's distinctive aroma. "Northern mountains?"

"Eastern foothills," he corrects, "Grows wild along the border. The Legion..." He stops abruptly, aware of revealing more than intended. "It's common knowledge in Rande."

Lukkar watches this exchange with barely concealed amusement, his eyes laughing even as he keeps his weathered face carefully neutral. "You two worked out your differences, I see." He stretches, joints popping audibly. "As for me, the wagon sits at their storehouse, it was emptied as soon as I arrived and is being filled now."

"You're not concerned about thieves?" Mardonius asks, genuinely curious. In most towns, valuable cargo would require guards through the night.

Lukkar's laugh carries a sharp edge. "Below my pay grade to oversee that business. Anyway, a thief in Swansbane would face the wrath of the locals long before I got my hands on them." He leans forward, voice dropping. "This town doesn't tolerate those who take from the community. Not when survival depends on every resource." His fingers drum against the wooden table. "Besides, where would they run? Into the forest at night?" He shakes his head. "Certain death."

The matter-of-fact delivery startles Mardonius more than any elaborate threat might have. Whatever lurks beyond Swansbane's walls after dark inspires more fear than the town's justice.

"We leave after sunrise?" Akantha asks, focussed entirely on direct need.

"Not too long after," Lukkar confirms. "Early, but not at first light. The gates open before dawn to let the morning patrols out." He glances toward the hall's entrance, where darkness is complete beyond the windows. "We'll be on our way with more than enough time to clear the wooded areas before nightfall."

"It doesn't matter if we reach Aissentur after dark?" Mardonius asks, noting the distinction.

"Different lands, different dangers," Lukkar shrugs. "The road to Aissentur is safe enough after you leave the forest. Bandits are the worst you'll face there, and they rarely cause problems that close to town." His expression darkens slightly. "Here, though... Well, you know the story, best be behind walls before night falls."

The serving girl who brought their ale earlier approaches their table. "The sleeping quarters are ready," she announces with no preamble and no particular inflection. "Follow."

They gather their belongings, Mardonius ensuring the brass case remains secure against his ribs. The common room has almost completely emptied now, there are only a few stragglers finishing meals or their drinks at the widely spaced tables. The serving girl leads them through a side entrance and down a short hallway lined with doors set at regular intervals.

"Communal sleeping room," she explains, opening the last door to reveal a chamber filled with straw-stuffed pallets arranged in neat rows. "Clean blanket provided. Water in the pitcher. Chamber pot beneath. Wash room two doors down on your right." Her instructions complete, she steps aside to allow them entry.

The room holds twenty sleeping places, though only a handful show signs of occupation. Small personal items mark claimed spaces, there is a folded cloak here, a pair of worn boots there. Most of the pallets remain empty, suggesting that many of Swansbane's residents sleep elsewhere.

"Not much privacy," Mardonius observes, selecting two pallets near the far wall, away from the door but with clear sightlines to it.

"Privacy is a luxury few can afford here," Lukkar says from the doorway. His outline stands stark against the lamplight from the hallway behind him. "Rest well. You've earned it after today's adventure."

He turns to leave, then pauses, one hand on the doorframe. A strange laugh escapes him, it is not the hearty chuckle of genuine amusement but something tighter, almost nervous. "One thing," he adds, half turning back to face them. "Don't sleep too deeply. If the bell sounds in the night, make your way to the walls..."

Before either can question this cryptic instruction, Lukkar is gone, his footsteps receding down the hallway with haste. The serving girl follows, closing the door behind her with a soft click that somehow sounds like finality.

Mardonius and Akantha exchange glances in the dimly lit room, neither needing to speak the question hanging between them: What happens when the bell sounds?

"Choose sleep spots?" Akantha suggests, breaking the tension with her 'here and now' attitude.

They arrange their meagre belongings on adjacent pallets, maintaining the seeds of cooperation that have developed since their encounter with the Fisher Folk. Neither mentions Lukkar's warning directly, yet it shapes their preparations. Weapons are placed within easy reach, footwear positioned for quick donning, cloaks laid on top for warmth. They individually head out for a quick wash but both choose to sleep this night in their leathers.

Other occupants filter in gradually, each nodding silent acknowledgment before claiming their own spaces. No one speaks above a whisper. No one lingers in conversation. Each person performs their night-time rituals with the same single-minded intensity that characterises all activity in Swansbane.

Mardonius stretches out on his pallet, the straw crackling beneath his weight as he finds a comfortable position. Sleep will come despite his unease; years in the Legion taught him to rest whenever opportunity allowed. Beside him, Akantha settles with her back to him, but he notices her eyes remain open, fixed on the door.

"Rest," he murmurs.

Her only response is a slight relaxation of her shoulders, but Mardonius recognises the concession. In that small surrender to fatigue, he glimpses something beyond their tactical alliance, the first fragile sprout of what soldiers know matters more than skill: mutual respect based on trusting that the other has got your back.

Outside, Swansbane prepares for another night behind its walls, archers and guards are patrolling, torches burn at regular intervals along the parapet. Whatever threat they anticipate remains invisible to Mardonius, yet he feels its presence like a weight pressing down from the darkness beyond.

CHAPTER 12

The bell's jarring clang tears through darkness, an iron voice calling danger. Mardonius' eyes snap open before his mind fully wakes, body already moving with a soldier's instinct for survival. Sleep falls away like an unwanted cloak as his hand finds his mace beside the pallet, fingers closing around the familiar grip before conscious thought can form. The common room erupts into silent purposeful movement but completely devoid of any panic.

"It's time," Akantha says. She is already on her feet, buckling her small shield onto her arm. She'd slept in her leather armour just as he had, heeding Lukkar's cryptic warning.

Mardonius stands and casts an eye over everyone else as he takes up his kit. The common room's other occupants, there are six in total, are pulling on boots and grabbing weapons as calmly as if this were a drill. A grey-haired woman checks a younger man's sword belt, her gnarled fingers working with surprising dexterity. Two middle-aged men strap shields to their arms in perfect synchronisation, but share no words. Across the room, a teenage girl secures her hair in to a pony tail before taking up a spear taller than herself.

No fear stains their faces, only concentration and complete focus on the task at hand. This, Mardonius realises, is routine for them.

"My longbow," he mutters to himself, reaching for the leather case propped beside his pack. He quickly retrieves his quiver, counting the arrows by touch; ten in total, precious few for a fight of any significance.

Akantha has already gathered her weapons. She makes for the door. "We follow."

Beyond the common room, the hallway teems with activity. More townspeople emerge from adjacent rooms, forming a steady stream toward the main exit. Their faces all bear the same calm expression. There is certainly no fear but neither is there any excitement. Mardonius has seen workers beginning a day of backbreaking labour showing more emotion than these people.

Outside, moonlight bathes Swansbane in silvery illumination. It transforms the town into a landscape of sharp contrasts, of deep shadows beside comparatively brilliant highlights. Torches and lanterns burn along the walls, marking the defensive perimeter like earthbound stars. The night air carries a bite of early spring chill, but Mardonius barely notices the cold.

The streets have become rivers of movement, all flowing toward the walls. Older men and women, those whose fighting days have passed, check weapons and armour as younger folk stroll past. Each person knows their role without instruction, a battle plan executed from muscle memory rather than command.

"The centre wall," a passing townsman says, noticing their hesitation. He points toward the northern section. "All capable bows there." He continues without waiting for acknowledgment, already focused on his own duty.

They join the current of defenders, Mardonius noting how age dictates function in this peculiar army. Adults of fighting age move with determined strides toward the walls, weapons ready. Teenagers carry bundles of arrows and extra weapons, distributing them at regular intervals. And then there is the children...

Mardonius watches a group of small children, none older than seven or eight, carrying water skins and bandages with solemn concentration. A boy who can't be more than six staggers under the weight of an arrow bundle, his face scrunched with the effort but eyes bright with importance. To them, this midnight alarm is a game they've played countless times, each knowing their part by heart.

"Like village attack drill," Akantha observes, her voice low as they walk. "But real."

Mardonius recognising the pattern of it all from his military experience. "Everyone knows their place." It is, however, the organisation that impresses him more than any show of martial prowess could. The very best-trained Legion units still required officers barking orders during night attacks, even units that have been in static defensive positions for years. Here, the defence operates silently, each component moving in concert without visible command.

They reach the stairs leading to the parapet, two among the steady flow of archers ascending. The stone steps, worn smooth by countless feet, rise at a gentle angle that allows quick movement without risking falls in the darkness. At the top, the wall stretches in both directions, its width sufficient for defenders to move freely behind the protective crenulations.

Mardonius takes position at an empty section of wall, setting his wrapped bow against the wall carefully before peering outward. The cleared ground before Swansbane stretches like a blank canvas in the moonlight, each shadow and depression visible from this height. Beyond the killing field, the forest looms; a wall of darkness more absolute than the night sky above.

An older man with a captain's bearing moves along the wall, checking positions without issuing orders. When he reaches Mardonius, his eyes flick to the longbow case with interest before meeting Mardonius' gaze.

"You'll want the north-eastern corner, stranger," he says, pointing to a section of wall to their right offering a wider field of view. "Best sight lines."

"Thank you," Mardonius responds, gathering his gear. The man's expertise is evident in the suggestion, the position would indeed maximise the longbow's range advantage.

As they move to the indicated spot, Mardonius observes the defenders settling into their places. Unlike the chaotic scramble he's witnessed at other settlements under attack, Swansbane's response feels choreographed, as if each person has a pre-ordained spot. Even now, with time to wait and time to think, there are no signs of tension.

"How many times have they done this before," he murmurs to Akantha as they reach their assigned position.

"Many times many." She replies, her eyes already scanning the darkness beyond the walls.

The moonlight catches her profile, highlighting the sharp angles of her face and the readiness in her posture. For all this morning's coldness, she now stands in her element, as a proud warrior prepared for battle.

Mardonius turns his attention outward again. The night air feels electric with anticipation. His mouth goes dry, his hearing sharpens. He can make out individual breaths along the wall now. A traveling bard he'd once shared a wineskin with had named this feeling with a wry smile: "Soldier's stage fright," that peculiar nervous alertness preceding violence.

The warning bell falls silent, its job complete. In its place comes a deeper quiet; it is the held breath before combat, the moment when possibility hangs suspended between preparation and action. All along the wall, defenders wait with arrows nocked and spears ready, their faces illuminated by torchlight into masks of determination.

Whatever comes from the darkness, this night Swansbane stands ready.

The parapet stretches to their left and right like the spine of some ancient beast. Mardonius feels the wooden planks through his boots as his eyes scan the emptiness beyond the walls. Moonlight bathes the cleared ground in silver, transforming ordinary terrain into something otherworldly. The night holds its breath, waiting.

Swansbane's walls stand twenty feet high, offering clear sight lines across the killing field to the forest's edge. The moon, nearly full tonight, casts enough light to distinguish movement at a considerable distance, yet shadows pool in depressions and furrows, creating perfect hiding places for advancing enemies. Mardonius notes these darker patches with a veteran's eye, marking potential threat points from long habit.

The cold presses against his skin, seeping through leather armour to chill the sweat forming beneath. His breath emerges in faint clouds that dissipate quickly in the night air. Along the wall, torch flames dance in the intermittent breeze, casting flickering light across the faces of defenders.

"Good position," Akantha murmurs beside him, her body angled to watch both the field and the activity along the wall. Her spear rests against the stone, within easy reach but leaving her hands free for now. "Clear shots."

Mardonius takes a knee to unwrap his longbow from its protective oiled cloth. The familiar ritual steadies him, focusing his thoughts as fingers trace the smooth ash surface, checking for any damage or weakness. The bow has served him through years of military service, its weight and balance as familiar as his own heartbeat. He runs his fingers along the string, feeling for frays or weak points before testing its tension.

Standing now he braces the lower limb of the bow against his foot before bending the upper limb. The ash flexes reluctantly, its resistance a testament to its power. The string slides into the nock with a satisfying click, transforming the separate components into a unified weapon. He plucks the string once, listening to its taut hum; the deadly sound of potential energy waiting to be released.

Beside him, Akantha approaches one of the defenders, a matronly hearth woman. "Need one," she states simply, gesturing to indicate a bow. "Can shoot."

The woman studies her briefly, assessing competence with experienced eyes before agreeing. "Riso," she calls to a man further along the wall. "Spare a bow for the outsider. She knows her business."

The man produces a spare bow from a rack built into the wall's interior face, along with a small quiver of arrows. He hands them to Akantha without comment, his attention already returning to the darkness beyond the wall.

Akantha tests the weapon with quick, competent movements, examining the pull and sighting along an arrow before grinning with satisfaction. She positions herself beside Mardonius, her stance revealing archery skills he hadn't previously observed. The bow is shorter than ideal for her height, but she adjusts naturally, compensating for its limitations.

"Takaz'Ran learn young," she says, noting his interest. "Before knife, before spear."

Mardonius reaches for his quiver, lamenting how few arrows he has for what is sizing up to be a prolonged engagement. Before he voices his concern movement catches his eye. A small figure approaches along the wall, struggling under the weight of a sizable arrow bundle.

A girl, perhaps four or five years old, makes her determined way toward them. Her dark hair is bound in tight braids that won't catch on bowstrings, and she wears a miniature version of the leather armour favoured by adult defenders. The arrow bundle in her arms seems almost as large as she is, yet she carries it with a sense of responsibility.

She stops before Mardonius, looking up with eyes that hold none of the fear he'd expect from a child her age during a night attack. Instead, there's only earnest determination. She offers a bundle to him.

"For the longbow," she says, her voice high and clear against the night's silence. "Twenty arrows. Good ones. I helped make them me'self"

Mardonius squats down to accept the offering, genuinely touched by the gesture. "Thank you," he says, keeping his voice gentle despite the tension of imminent battle. The arrows are indeed quality work; straight shafts, proper fletching, sharp steel points that would pierce most armour with ease. "These are excellent arrows indeed. Thank you."

The girl's eyes widen as she studies his bow. "It's beautiful," she whispers, one small hand reaching toward it before stopping respectfully short of touching. "Did you make it?"

"No," he replies, adding the new arrows to his quiver. "It was a gift."

She nods as if this makes perfect sense, then offers a solemn smile. "The Lady will bless your aim tonight," she says with the certainty of absolute faith. "She protects Swansbane and we protect her."

The mention of 'The Lady' recalls the strange temple they'd visited earlier, with its unusual depiction of Lady Eanna as a watery fertility symbol rather than warrior. Before he can respond, the girl turns away, already moving toward another defender to perform her duty.

"Children know only this," Akantha observes quietly, watching the girl go. "Born to battle."

Mardonius feels a heaviness at this. These children have never known peace, their entire existence is shaped by whatever threat lurks beyond the walls. Their games are preparations for war, their education focused on survival. It reminds him too much of border villages he'd seen during his service, places where childhood ended before it truly began.

He pushes away the heaviness of those thoughts and lifts his bow, feeling the worn grip against his palm, his fingers find their place on the string. In the army, nineteen archers in his Tent, then the full eighty in his Wagon, had once looked to him for orders. Now, as his breath steadies, he allows Mardonius the soldier to emerge from beneath Mardonius the wanderer.

Along the wall, dozens of defenders make their own final weapon checks, or adjustments to their armour. There are isolated murmurings of quiet conversation even while eyes remain fixed on the darkness beyond. Torchlight catches on metal points of arrows and spears, creating pinpoints of fierce light amid the shadows.

The wait stretches, time measured in heartbeats and slow breaths. Mardonius settles his breathing, controlling his heart rate though willpower as he was taught long ago.

"There," Akantha says suddenly, her voice barely above a whisper as she points toward the forest edge. "Movement."

Mardonius follows her gesture, eyes straining against the darkness. For a moment, he sees nothing but shadows and moonlight. Then, there, a shifting darkness against the deeper black of the trees. Something emerges from the forest's edge, followed by others. Their forms still too distant to identify clearly, but they are unmistakably moving with purpose toward Swansbane's walls.

"They come," murmurs a defender nearby. Similar whispers travel along the wall, a ripple of recognition rather than alarm.

Mardonius nocks an arrow, the motion smooth and instinctive. His shoulders settle, and the earlier jitters dissolve into the familiar calm that always arrives when combat becomes inevitable. At his side, Akantha's lips move in quiet rhythm, her native tongue forming what might be prayer or battle-poem, the cadence rising and falling as she centres herself, in her own way, for what approaches.

The parapet falls into complete silence as defenders wait with bows and spears at the ready. In that suspended moment between preparation and action, Mardonius feels an unexpected kinship with these strange, determined people who face the darkness with such grim familiarity.

The creatures emerge from the forest's edge like nightmares taking physical form. Moonlight reveals them in stages; first as darker shapes against darkness, then as distinct silhouettes advancing across the open ground. They move unevenly toward Swansbane's walls, spread out rather than bunched, attacking simultaneously but without coordination. He counts fifteen distinct shapes materialising from the darkness. Mardonius' eyes flicks from one to another, categorising threats by size and movement.

"Seventy feet and closing," murmurs a defender nearby, voice steady as he counts down the distance. No commands to hold echo along the wall; each defender knows the effective range of their weapons, when to draw and when to loose. If only the recruits he once trained had this level of discipline, he mused, what a force they would have been.

Mardonius can begin to identify the enemy now. Nine smaller forms lope forward with a hunched, jerking gait he recognises immediately: Goblins, their mottled greenish-brown skin catching moonlight in leprous patches. They wear little more than loincloths, their wiry bodies covered in ritual scars and crude tattoos. Rusty weapons glint in their hands, a mixture of short bows, spears, and clubs studded with metal fragments.

Goblins are common enough Twisted that any experienced fighter knows their weaknesses: poor coordination and terrible aim but dangerous in numbers due to their feral tenacity.

Behind the vanguard lumbers a much larger figure, towering over them at nearly eight feet tall with pallid, bleached-white skin stretched over massive muscles. It moves with ponderous steps, squinting against even the modest moonlight, one huge hand dragging a club that appears fashioned from an entire tree trunk bound with metal bands. Mardonius has never encountered such a creature, but its nature is clear from its proportions and movements, it is a brutish force of simple destruction.

"Cave Ogre," hisses a defender to his right, giving the creature a name. "Rare to see one above ground."

Five figures with unnaturally elongated limbs scramble across the ground with disturbing speed. These he knows; Fisher Folk, unmistakable with their pale, translucent skin and webbed extremities. Mardonius feels Akantha tense beside him, her recent wounds from their underground encounter still fresh beneath her bandage. That is not what bothers her though, "They never come like this. Together," she states under her breath, confusion evident as she shakes her head. "Different species. More like to kill each other."

Mardonius has no answer for this unusual coalition, so he focused instead on the immediate threat. The Goblins reach fifty feet from the wall and split their tactics. Three nock arrows to their primitive short bows while five continue their charge toward the base of the wall, brandishing melee weapons and screeching challenges that sound more like animal noises than language.

The Goblin archers loose a volley but it is a pathetic effort that falls well short of the wall. Their second attempt flies higher but still harmlessly impacts the solid logs several feet below the defenders. Mardonius nearly dismisses them as irrelevant when something at the rear of the group catches his full attention.

One Goblin hangs back, standing twenty feet behind its fellows. Unlike the others, this one wears elaborate decorations, it has bones threaded through pierced ears, a necklace of small skulls, and a headdress of feathers and teeth that adds a foot to its height. It carries no bow or club but instead grips a gnarled staff topped with a crystalline object that captures and refracts moonlight in unnatural patterns.

Mardonius' blood runs cold with recognition. "Magic user," he says, the words emerging as a whisper before he draws breath to shout. "MAGIC USER! REAR RANK!"

Heads turn along the wall, defenders following his pointing gesture to identify this new threat. Mardonius' warning carries the bitter weight of experience. During his decade with the Legion, he'd witnessed firsthand the devastation a single spell-caster could unleash on unprepared troops.

The memory surfaces unbidden. It was a skirmish along the eastern border, a Goblin shaman similar to this one hid among rocks whilst its kin engaged the Legion's front line. They'd spotted the creature too late, watched helplessly as it cast a sickly yellow-green spell that washed over ten of his comrades from a spear unit. Their screams still echo in his nightmares; the sound of good soldiers dying as their flesh decayed while still on their bones, a process that should take weeks compressed into agonising minutes.

"Loose at will!" calls a confident voice further along the wall.

Mardonius is already drawing his bow, the ash flexing smoothly as he pulls the string to his ear in one fluid motion. The Goblin shaman stands partially obscured by its advancing allies, the distance and darkness making it a challenging target even for a skilled archer like him. He exhales slowly, steadying his aim, focusing on the elaborate headdress that makes the creature more visible than its kin.

All along the wall, defenders draw and aim. The night air fills with the distinctive sound of bowstrings being pulled taut, the collective creak of wood under tension forming a strange harmony. Mardonius feels the hair on his arms and neck rise, it is not just from the imminent violence, but from the unmistakable prickling sensation that accompanies gathering magical energy.

The Goblin shaman has begun its casting, spindly arms raised overhead, the crystal atop its staff glowing with an unnatural inner light. Mardonius can see its lips moving in strange patterns, uttering words that would damage a human throat if spoken. The air around it seems to waver, like heat rising from sun-baked stone, but with an oily, unclean quality that disturbs the eye.

"Shoot it!" Akantha hisses beside him, her own bow already drawn and aimed at one of the charging Goblins. "Now!"

He releases his arrow, feeling the string snap against his protected wrist, the shaft leaving his bow with a sound like a bird taking flight. The arrow arcs through the night, a briefly visible streak against the darkness before it vanishes from sight. A moment later comes the dull thud of impact. Unfortunately it is not the solid strike of a hit, but the softer sound of an arrow embedding itself in earth.

A miss. The target is too distant and too small.

Cursing under his breath, Mardonius reaches for another arrow, his movements steady despite the urgency pounding in his chest. Sixty paces is at the extreme edge of effective range in darkness, but the consequences of allowing the shaman to complete its casting are unacceptable. Each muttered syllable brings it closer to successfully unleashing whatever horror it is conjuring.

However, this is also the time when it is most vulnerable. He'd seen it before, the moment when a spell caster's concentration wavers, be it an arrow or shout shattering their focus, it can make the whole spell fizzle out or even send the arcane energies spiralling back upon their summoner. Now is that precious window; that brief vulnerability before the magic solidifies into something unstoppable.

Along the wall, other arrows fly toward the approaching creatures. Several find their marks, Goblins stumble and fall, their high-pitched screams cutting through the night air. But the most dangerous target remains untouched, the shaman continues to focus its mana with growing intensity.

The massive Cave Ogre bellows some distance to the left as an arrow strikes its shoulder, it sounds more annoyed than in pain. Its pace increases and is surprisingly fast for a creature of such bulk. The Fisher Folk spread out, their unnatural limbs allowing them to cover ground with disturbing speed, they are already halfway to the right side of the wall.

Mardonius nocks his second arrow, drawing and aiming in one smooth motion. Beside him, Akantha murmurs something in her native tongue, a prayer or curse he can't tell which. The Goblin shaman's staff now glows with sickly green light, illuminating its misshapen features from below, transforming its face into a grotesque mask of malevolent purpose.

His finger releases the string, sending another arrow hurtling toward the distant threat, even as he reaches for a third shaft. The battle has begun all along the wall in earnest, but Mardonius sees only one enemy, the magic user whose death must come before any other consideration.

Mardonius' second arrow flies wide, skimming past the Goblin wizard's shoulder to disappear into the darkness beyond. The distance is proving challenging even for his trained eye and steady hand. Frustration surges through him, hot and sharp, each missed shot allows the creature more time to complete its casting, bringing whatever terrible magic it wields closer to fruition.

"Third shaft," he mutters, fingers finding another arrow without looking. The familiar ritual of nock-draw-aim steadies his racing thoughts, narrowing his focus to the single point of the goblin shaman.

Beside him, Akantha has shifted her attention to the larger threats. Her bow sings as she looses an arrow at one of the largest goblins, striking it in the thigh. The creature barely registers the hit, continuing its frantic advance with single-minded determination. She mutters phrases in her native tongue between shots. He is willing to bet they are not prayers for success but vows of vengeance directed at the approaching abominations.

All along the wall, bows twang in a staggered rhythm, a deadly music composed of tension and release. Arrows rain down on the approaching creatures, many finding their marks despite the challenging conditions. The defenders choosing targets based on position and opportunity rather than requiring specific orders.

Three Goblins already lie motionless on the moonlit ground, their crude charges ended by well-placed arrows. A fourth drags itself forward despite a shaft protruding from its shoulder, snarling defiance with each painful movement. Away to the right the Fisher Folk prove more difficult targets, their unnaturally elongated limbs allowing jerking, unpredictable movements that cause arrows to miss or strike non-vital areas.

Mardonius sees none of this as he draws his bow a third time, focusing entirely on the Goblin shaman. The creature has stopped moving, its attention fixed on completing its casting. The crystalline focus atop its staff now pulses with sickly green light, illuminating the surrounding area with an unnatural glow that seems to corrupt the clean silver of moonlight. The Goblin's lips spit out words of evil and its free hand weaves symbols in the air that leave momentary trails of luminescence.

He exhales slowly, steadying his aim, compensating for distance and the slight breeze that has begun to stir the night air. This arrow flies true, its path a perfect arc toward the target. But at the last moment, the shaman shifts position, leaning forward to complete some crucial gesture in its casting. The shaft passes through empty air where its chest had been a heartbeat before.

"No! Mardonius hisses in anguish, reaching for a fourth arrow even as he recognises it will come too late. The shaman's spell has reached its culmination, the green nimbus between its hands coalescing into something tangible; a roiling, toxic cloud that hovers momentarily before the creature like a held breath.

With a final gesture of triumph, the wizard pushes the deadly magic forward. The cloud accelerates toward the wall, moving faster than any natural fog, its trajectory aimed directly at the clustered defenders. Mardonius suspects the spell is not the flesh-rotting horror he witnessed years ago, but a poison cloud that will incapacitate or kill anyone who breathes its vapours.

"Down!" he shouts, preparing to drop below the wall's protection.

Before he can move, the night air splits with a sound like tearing silk.

A spear of brilliant blue light streaks from somewhere along the wall, so bright it leaves a burning afterimage on Mardonius' vision. The magical projectile moves with impossible speed, crossing the distance to the shaman in less time than it takes to draw breath. It strikes the creature squarely in the chest, punching through its body with devastating force.

For one suspended moment, the Goblin stands frozen, illuminated from within by the blue energy that has pierced it. Its toxic cloud dissipates instantly, unravelling into harmless wisps that fade into the night air. Then the creature topples backward, the ornate staff falling from lifeless fingers, body already beginning to crumble into ash as the foreign magic consumes it from inside.

Mardonius turns toward the source of this unexpected salvation. Thirty paces away stands the priestess from the temple, her blue robes now replaced by silver armour that catches moonlight like water. Her arms remain extended in the final position of her casting, fingers splayed and head thrown back. Where the Goblin's magic had seemed to corrupt the air around it, hers appears to purify, leaving a scent like rainfall on stone in its wake.

Her face, serene during the temple ritual, now carries an expression of fierce contempt as she stares at the spot where her counterpart fell. "For the Lady of the Secret Waters!" she cries, her voice carrying clearly across the wall. "Swansbane stands!"

"SWANSBANE STANDS!" The defenders roar in response, the unified sound crashing against the night like a breaking wave. This is the most overt display of emotion Mardonius has seen since arriving in this village and yet the declaration carries no triumph, only grim determination and absolute certainty.

With the magical threat eliminated, the battle transforms from potential disaster to methodical slaughter. The remaining attackers continue their charge, but without supernatural support, they face the full, unhindered force of Swansbane's defences.

The massive Cave Ogre reaches the base of the wall, swinging its club against the logs with enough force to send vibrations through the structure. But the angle prevents effective strikes, and concentrated arrow fire finds the vulnerable points in its massive frame – eyes, throat, the softer flesh beneath its arms. After absorbing a dozen shafts, it collapses in a heap, its final roar cut short by an arrow through its open mouth.

The Fisher Folk fare no better. Their climbing abilities might have made them dangerous if they'd reached the walls, but concentrated fire drops them one by one, their pale bodies crumpling beneath volleys that rely on volume rather than precision. Their unnatural flexibility, an advantage in the confined tunnel where Mardonius and Akantha had fought them earlier, provides no defence against arrows fired *en masse*.

Mardonius shifts his attention to the remaining Goblins, choosing a target that has almost reached the wall. He draws and releases in one fluid motion, his arrow taking the creature through the eye. It drops without sound, one more shadow returning to the darkness from which it emerged.

Beside him, Akantha looses shaft after shaft, her expression cold and focused. Each time a Goblin is hit by her arrows, her lips curl in a satisfied grimace. She's working through personal demons with each shot.

The battle, if it can even be called such, lasts less than ten minutes from first sighting to final kill. When the last creature falls, a Goblin attempting to climb the wall, a different bell sounds three times, signalling the all-clear. Defenders lower their bows but maintain their positions, eyes still scanning the darkness beyond the wall for any movement.

"They sent a wizard," says a defender with a crooked nose, her nasal voice thoughtful rather than frightened. "Not seen that in a while."

"Wonder where that Cave Troll came from," adds another. "They're getting desperate."

Mardonius counts his remaining arrows: sixteen, including those from his quiver and those provided by the young girl. One Goblin confirmed dead. Not his best performance, but acceptable given the challenging conditions. More concerning is what the Akantha noted, the unusual cooperation among typically solitary Twisted species, and the presence of a magic user in what was otherwise an essentially pointless raid.

The priestess has already departed, returning to the temple without seeking acknowledgment for her decisive intervention. Several defenders touch their foreheads in a gesture of respect as she passes, but she acknowledges none of them, her focus apparently turned inward after the expenditure of mana.

"Always like this?" Mardonius asks the nearest defender, a middle-aged man with a paunch who looked more like a doting father than a fierce defender.

"The attacks? Yes, most nights." The man inspects his bowstring for wear as he speaks. "It was a small one tonight and the magic is uncommon. But almost always something." He glances toward the temple, visible on the hill above them. "The Lady protects us. As we protect her waters."

Before Mardonius can question this cryptic statement, a different bell sounds, the single, sustained tone that signals the rotation of watch duty. Fresh defenders arrive to replace those who have fought, the transition occurring with the same pragmatism as everything else in Swansbane.

The battle may have ended with the last Goblin's death-cry but the night stretches before them like an unfinished scroll. This strange town of Swansbane, with its silver-armoured priestess and too-practiced defenders, has offered him nothing but riddles wrapped in bloodshed.

The common room feels different upon their return, smaller somehow, its shadows deeper despite the lamps that burn at half-flame along the walls. Mardonius' muscles carry the familiar ache that follows combat, not from exertion, that soreness will come tomorrow, but from the sustained tension of holding readiness for too long. He places his longbow back in its case with respect, fingers lingering on the smooth ash surface before wrapping the oiled cloth carefully around it.

Akantha sits heavily on her pallet, unlacing her bracer. The bandage around her upper arm is still intact though the bruise would be sore after all that shooting. As he expected, she ignores it, focused instead on the routine of post-battle equipment check. Her borrowed bow had been returned to Swansbane's armoury, her own weapons arranged within easy reach beside her bedding.

"Clean shot," she says unexpectedly, glancing up at Mardonius. "The one you took. Between eyes."

He gives a slight bow, accepting the rare compliment for what it is; a warrior's acknowledgment of another's skill. "Saw you get a nice big one. Upper chest, angled toward the heart. Good placement."

The exchange feels ritualistic, a way of processing what they've experienced through shared professional assessment.

"Town people fight well," Akantha observes, her tone neutral and words carefully chosen. "Like soldiers. Not militia."

"They've had enough experience," Mardonius agrees, remembering the uncanny discipline of the defence, the absence of panic or disorder even when faced with magical attack. "Years of it, I'd guess."

The door to the common room swings open, admitting a figure that takes Mardonius a moment to recognise despite its face. Lukkar stands before them, but not the slovenly wagon driver who had guided them from Aissentur. This Lukkar stands straight-backed and confident, his previous hunched posture entirely absent. Instead of the stained tunic and battered quilted armour, he wears well-maintained ring mail over leathers. A short sword hangs at his hip, its scabbard showing the polished care of a weapon regularly used and cleaned.

Most striking is his face, the vacant, slightly dull expression replaced by sharp intelligence and barely contained energy. Even his speech patterns have transformed, the lazy country drawl giving way to clipped, precise syllables.

"Well fought!" he declares, striding into the room with the confident gait of a man comfortable in his own skin. His eyes gleam with an almost feverish light, the aftermath of battle-energy still coursing through him. "Quite the show tonight, wasn't it?"

Mardonius straightens, reassessing everything he thought he knew about their guide. The transformation is too complete to be coincidental: Lukkar has been playing a role from the moment they met, for reasons that remain unclear.

"You look different," Akantha states bluntly, never one to dance around niceties.

Lukkar laughs, the sound is rich and genuine. "Different occasions, different appearances." He gestures to his armour with casual pride. "No sense ruining good equipment on the dusty road, is there? Besides, travellers respond better to simple folk than to armed men."

He crosses to Mardonius, clapping him on the shoulder with startling familiarity. "Well Wagon, what did you think of that! Great fun! A pity that a few groups managed to make it down the Quay road, but at least the town is safe, eh?"

"Quay road?" Mardonius questions, latching onto the detail that might provide insight into Swansbane's mysteries.

"The old path down to the river," Lukkar explains, his excitement dimming slightly as he moves from post-battle euphoria to information giver. "Twisted try for it every time. Seems they want what's below more than what's up here." He shrugs, the gesture dismissive. "Don't get me wrong. They are serious in the attacks on the town, Villagers cannot afford to ignore them, but there is always a larger number heading for the steep stairs down to the Quay."

Mardonius remembers the ancient crane mechanisms they'd observed earlier, the sense that something important once existed, perhaps still exists, at the bottom of the cliff where the river flows. Lukkar's casual mention suggests the attackers have some specific objective beyond simply raiding Swansbane.

"What's down there that they want?" he asks directly.

"Now _that_", he emphasises, "is a very pretty question."

Lukkar stretches, armour clinking softly with the movement. "Rest up, we leave at dawn. Meet me at the east gate as the sun breaks the horizon. Get what sleep you can."

Lukkar turns to leave, then pauses at the door, his expression softening into something more genuine.

"You both did well tonight. Not everyone would stand the wall their first night here." A hint of respect enters his voice. "Swansbane remembers those who defend it."

Then he's gone, the door closing behind him with soft finality. Mardonius and Akantha exchange glances, the question hanging between them: What exactly have they stumbled into?

"Something wrong here," Akantha says finally, voicing what they both feel. "Town. Attacks, Lukkar. It all wrong."

Mardonius settles onto his pallet. The brass case from the Fisher Folk lair remains secured against his ribs, their official mission technically complete. But Swansbane has inserted itself into their journey as an unexpected complication, a mystery neither of them anticipated.

"We leave at dawn," he says, echoing Lukkar's instruction while privately wondering if departure will be as simple as it sounds. "One night only."

Akantha lies back on her bedding, one hand resting on the knife beside her pillow. "One night too many."

He stares at the ceiling, listening to the sounds of Swansbane settling after battle. Muted conversations, the distant clang of weapons being cleaned and stored, occasional footsteps passing outside their door. There are no celebrations, no bragging contests, all the normal sounds expected after a fight. Instead there are only normal sounds, in a place that defies normality. The town just rolls over and goes back to sleep with the certainty that more attacks will come.

Tomorrow they'll leave this strange, besieged settlement, carrying its secrets with them like unwanted souvenirs. But tonight, they remain within its walls, part of its defence, connected to its mysteries in ways neither fully understands.

Sleep comes slowly, and when it does, his dreams are filled with pale creatures climbing down endless stairs, seeking something that waits below, something Swansbane defends with the determination of the truly desperate.

CHAPTER 13

15th Day of Spring

Morning light filters through the ancient oak canopy, dappling the road with shifting patterns of gold and shadow. Mardonius inhales deeply, savouring air untainted by the acrid smoke of burning Twisted corpses that had permeated Swansbane at dawn. As expected his muscles ache from the yesterday's exertions, but the pain feels like a warrior's comfort rather than a burden. The wagon's steady rumble beneath the wooden wheels creates a hypnotic rhythm, but he does not let it lure him into complacency.

They've travelled far enough that Swansbane's walls have disappeared beyond the gentle curve of the forest road. In their place, spring unfolds in quiet splendour. Wild violets carpet the verges in patches of purple, the morning birdsong filters through the trees. He takes heart in this, nature's proof that no Twisted lurk nearby, birds know better than to sing where corruption walks.

Mardonius rolls his shoulders, working out the stiffness from last night's archery. His quiver and coin purse both have more weight to them, each a blessing he'd never have expected to acquire in an isolated outpost like Swansbane. The brass scroll case still presses against his ribs beneath his leather armour, their mission's tangible success nestled close to his heart.

Ahead of the wagon, Akantha rides Ferzif'Eanna with her usual straight-backed dignity, despite the donkey's less-than-impressive stature and occasional comical braying. She maintains enough distance to claim independence while staying close enough to catch any conversation. The bruise on her arm has darkened overnight into a mottled purple-black map of yesterday's battle, yet she shows gives no sign of discomfort beyond favouring her other arm.

"The beast's name means 'Shield of Eanna'," Lukkar explains, as Mardonius' watches Akantha and her mount. "Ambitious name for a donkey, but the Takaz'Ran never name anything lightly. Her nickname for it, 'FerFer', is also their word for the sound a bull makes before charging. It is probably the biggest concession to humour she is ever likely to make."

Lukkar sits taller today, his hunched, shambling persona discarded like an ill-fitting garment. The transformation extends beyond mere posture, his eyes are sharper, his movements precise where before they'd been exaggerated and clumsy. The stained, torn quilted armour has been replaced with well-oiled leather that fits his frame perfectly, suggesting custom craftsmanship rather than standard issue. A short sword is openly scabbarded at his belt, its worn grip and polished pommel telling the story of a weapon regularly used and well-maintained. Beside him rests an ornate bow inlaid with pale wood.

The man who needed them as guards was a fiction. This version of Lukkar, alert, armed, professional, is the reality. Mardonius wonders how many other illusions from the past few days will unravel before they reach Aissentur.

"Good haul this trip," Lukkar comments, gesturing to the load behind them with a thumb. "Feywood and teak, straight from Swansbane's work yards. Master Gynn will turn a tidy profit indeed."

Mardonius studies the cargo more carefully. The planks lie stacked and secured with rope, their surfaces rich with distinctive grain patterns that even his untrained eye recognises as valuable. Feywood, so named for its value amongst the Fey, has an almost weightless quality despite its strength, it also glows with a subtle inner light when twilight touches it. The darker teak beside it seems to absorb light rather than reflect it, its density promising generations of use without deterioration. Together, they represent more wealth than Mardonius has seen in one place since leaving the Legion's service.

"Beautiful wood," Mardonius observes. "Perilous to get too."

Lukkar nods, pride evident in the gesture. "Swansbane may be strange, but its resources are unmatched in the north. They have access to wilds that most would not dare exploit." He pats the wooden seat beneath him. "Master Gynn could make a fortune running this routes alone."

The forest deepens around them as they continue east, the road narrowing slightly where less-travelled sections allow understory plants to encroach upon its edges. Sunlight penetrates the canopy at steeper angles now, creating bright corridors through the green gloom. Mardonius notes landmarks from their journey toward Swansbane, a lightning-split oak, a small stream crossing beneath an ancient stone bridge, but they seem different, ordinary rather than ominous.

His thoughts return to the night's battle, replaying the methodical defence of Swansbane's walls. The townspeople's combat prowess had impressed him professionally even as their silent acceptance of their situation disturbed him personally. A town under constant siege yet functioning like a dedicated military production centre. Children crafting arrows by day and delivering them by night, a priestess whose magic struck with lethal precision. A population that stood up to nightly attack yet built something resembling normality within their walls.

"Copper for your thoughts," Lukkar says, interrupting Mardonius' reflection. "Still dwelling on Swansbane?"

Mardonius considers deflection, then opts for honesty. "Never seen anything like it. A town that treats constant assaults like inclement weather."

Lukkar laughed at that but it contained no humour. "When something happens often enough, it becomes routine. Even death and monsters." He adjusts his grip on the reins, his eyes never sitting still as he scans the terrain ahead. "We'll make good time today. Should reach the halfway point by midday, Aissentur by sunset if we push, but I think it best to make our homecoming in the evening."

The path begins a more gradual descent, following the natural contours of the land as it winds toward the plains where Aissentur awaits. Through gaps in the forest, Mardonius catches glimpses of the Upper Gift River's relentless winding through the wilds. The sight brings unexpected comfort, a reminder that a normal world exists beyond Swansbane's bizarre isolation.

Mardonius finds himself breathing easier with each mile they put between themselves and the cliff-edged town. The lingering unease that had followed him from their communal sleeping quarters begins to dissipate and is replaced by cautious optimism. They have survived, completed their mission, and acquired unexpected wealth along the way.

Yet beneath this surface satisfaction, questions nag away at him. What secrets does Swansbane guard so fiercely? What drives the Twisted to attack night after night? And what awaits at the bottom of those ancient Quay steps that justifies such relentless assault?

For now, Mardonius is content to leave these mysteries behind them, at least physically. The answers, if they exist, can wait for safer surroundings and fuller purses. The morning stretches before them, beautiful in its ordinary peace, and that is enough.

The memory of their departure from Swansbane surfaces in Mardonius' mind as the wagon crests a small rise in the forest road. They had woken while stars still dominated the sky, roused not by any official summons but by the ingrained habit of sell-swords and warriors who know departures wait for no one. The common room held only their two occupied pallets; the other straw beds lay flattened and empty, their occupants already gone to morning duties. Only the lingering scent of smoke and sweat on their own bodies remained as evidence of last night's combat hours.

In the Food Hall a serving woman had appeared with wooden bowls of steaming gruel. It was a thick, grey porridge studded with fruit and nuts, and far more substantial than Mardonius had expected. She'd spoken no greeting, asked no questions about their rest, simply placed the food before them and walked off to other duties.

"Eat," Akantha said, already diving into her portion. "Long road."

They shovelled down the last of their breakfast, gathered their few belongings, and stepped outside into the biting air. Not one townsperson acknowledged their departure. There were no farewell waves, no curious glances, not even the casual disinterest of strangers passing strangers.

Outside, pre-dawn darkness still gripped the narrow streets, the lanterns and torches long extinguished. The air carried a bitter chemical tang, the smell of Twisted corpses beginning to decay, it was well-known that their unnatural flesh broke down much more rapidly than human remains. Mardonius had expected some disruption to the town's rhythm after such an attack, be it hurried repairs of damaged wall sections, wounded being tended, or perhaps even mourning for fallen defenders. Instead, he'd found a normal town beginning a normal day.

Outside the gate near the eastern wall, a work crew of four men and two women dragged Twisted corpses toward a deep pit away from the wall. They wore leather gloves and face coverings, protection against the corrupting effects of prolonged contact with Twisted flesh. Their movements carried no urgency, not even disgust, it was just another chore performed countless times before. One corpse, then another, arranged in the pit without any ceremony before being doused with oil from clay jugs.

As dawn's first light had painted the eastern sky in washed-out pinks and greys, Swansbane had stirred to life around them. Farm workers gathered tools and headed toward the cultivated fields just beyond the walls. Figures with fishing nets and spears moved towards paths leading down the eastern side of the cliff, obviously heading towards the Upper Gift River before it hit the falls. Hunters, distinguished by their forest-coloured leathers and bows, had already departed and were even now trudging towards the north-western forests.

Children emerged from dwellings, not to play but to assume their own roles in this strange community. Some carried water, others gathering bundles of arrows to replenish the previous night's expenditure. The youngest swept the streets or collected waste with the same solemn purpose that marked their elders. Nowhere did Mardonius see the casual idleness that characterised most settlements at dawn, no gossip clusters, no complaints about early risings, no one even stood to just take in the beauty of the coming sunrise.

"Like watching ants," Akantha had observed quietly, her voice barely audible. "Each knows task without being told."

Their path to the eastern gate had taken them past the temple that dominated Swansbane's central hill. Through this second viewing the structure's ancient origins became more apparent, weathered stone bearing architectural elements Mardonius couldn't identify, they were certainly too fluid in design for Randeri influence. Unlike the previous evening though, when they'd encountered only the priestess and her young assistant, the temple now hummed with activity.

From within its walls, voices rose in rhythmic chanting but these were not the martial hymns to Eanna the Warrior that Mardonius knew from military ceremonies, but something older, the words unintelligible yet making his heartbeat lift in sympathy at its cadence. The sound seemed to resonate from the stone itself, as if the building amplified and transformed the human voices into something more elemental.

At the temple's entrance, the same silver-armoured priestess who had destroyed the Goblin wizard with her spell now bent over a wounded townsman. Her hands glowed with soft blue light that transferred from her fingers to his injured shoulder, a healing spell. Three more wounded waited nearby, their expressions patient despite their pain. Unlike the frantic healing tents Mardonius remembered from battlefield campaigns, this scene projected serene confidence, both healer and healed were certain of the outcome.

Beside him, Akantha had made a sound, it was not quite a scoff, not quite a hiss, but her face tightened with something that might have been disapproval.

"What?" Mardonius had asked, catching her eye.

Akantha had glanced toward the temple entrance, where carved reliefs depicted flowing water emerging from a woman's body. "None of the images of blessed Lady Eanna make sense," she'd said, her tone suggesting she'd bitten back stronger words. Then she'd shrugged, a dismissive gesture that closed the subject as firmly as a slammed door.

The comment had lingered in Mardonius' mind as they'd continued toward the gate. His own religious education had been practical rather than theological. He knew Eanna as the warrior-judge who presided over soldiers and those who support them. She ruled over oaths and contracts and her blue star marked military standards and legal documents throughout Rande. The water-bearing figure in Swansbane's temple shared only the most superficial resemblance to the armoured goddess he recognised.

Yet something in Akantha's reaction suggested more than simple theological disagreement. The tension in her shoulders did not match the careful neutrality of her expression. He could not say he knew her mind and heart with any certainty but it read like the signs of someone encountering something that challenged fundamental beliefs. What had she seen in those carvings that disturbed her so deeply?

By the time they'd reached the gate, the wagon had been waiting, loaded with valuable timber and ready for departure. Lukkar had greeted them with a brisk wave that matched the town's overall demeanour. He checked the cargo one final time before gesturing them to make ready to depart. As they passed the massive gates into the full morning light, Mardonius had felt an almost physical relief at the prospect of leaving Swansbane behind.

Now, hours later on the forest road, the memory of that place still greatly unsettles him.

The wagon jolts over a protruding root, pulling Mardonius from his recollections of Swansbane. The sun has climbed higher now, fully burning away the morning mist that had clung to the low-lying forest floor. With Akantha riding several yards ahead, a rare moment of relative privacy presents itself. Mardonius shifts on the hard wooden seat, turning slightly toward Lukkar, whose attention remains fixed on guiding the horses through a narrower section of road.

"That place," Mardonius begins, keeping his voice low despite the isolation of the road, "Swansbane. It's like nothing I've ever seen before."

Lukkar's mouth quirks into a half-smile, though his eyes remain watchful of the path ahead. "Noticed that, did you?"

"Hard not to," Mardonius runs a hand along his quiver, feeling the reassuring outline of each arrow through the leather. "Children more mature than most adults I know. Everyone armed. Nightly battles treated like a dull but necessary chore." He pauses, watching Lukkar's expression. "Do you know why?"

The wagon driver, or whatever his true role might be, raises his hands in an elaborate shrug. "Truth? I don't know as much as I'd like." He checks over his shoulder, ensuring their cargo remains secure before continuing. "Made dozens of runs there over the years. Asked questions when I could. Got different answers each time, or, more often, none at all." His face turns serious. "Not sure even Master Gynn understands that place fully and he's been trading with them for over ten years."

A jay screams from a nearby oak, startling a rabbit that darts across the road before the horses. Lukkar adjusts the reins immediately, barely disrupting their steady pace. The moment stretches, and Mardonius wonders if this is all the explanation he'll receive.

"The attacks happen at least four nights a week," Lukkar finally continues, his voice taking on the matter-of-fact tone of a man discussing crop rotations rather than deadly assaults. "Usually more, almost never less. Always after full dark. Always the same pattern."

"Pattern?"

"Twisted throw themselves at the walls," Lukkar explains, gesturing with one hand to illustrate. "Different types attacking together, which isn't natural for them. They don't group up like that elsewhere. If anything, they would attack each other in the wilds." He shifts the reins to his other hand. "But here's the thing, the wall attacks are just a distraction. The defenders have to focus there, the very few times Twisted have got inside it has not been pretty. Meanwhile other groups of Twisted sneak around to the western side, toward the Quay Steps."

"The steps to the cliff base," Mardonius recalls the ancient crane mechanisms they'd observed, rusting monuments to some forgotten purpose.

"Exactly. There's a massive waterfall there where the Upper Gift River plunges over the cliff. It marks the beginning of the Lower Gift River." Lukkar's expression grows animated as he warms to his subject. "The Quay once served as a major trading post for the Chillisar Empire. Ships could sail upriver past many a temple-town, offload at the Quay, and goods would be winched up to Swansbane by those crane systems."

Mardonius pictures it. Vessels moored along stone docks, cargo rising up the sheer cliff face, commerce flowing through a settlement that now exists only as a shadow of its former importance. "What changed?"

"No one quite knows. Probably it was us wiping out the Chillisar. There are almost no records of the place from the time of the fall of their Empire. What few we have found suggest the attacks began centuries ago, gradually increasing until regular trade became impossible. Swansbane just fell off the maps around then." Lukkar navigates around a fallen branch without breaking his narrative rhythm. "The cranes were dismantled about seventy years back, not because they'd rusted beyond repair, but because Twisted kept using them to infiltrate the town."

The tactical logic makes immediate sense to Mardonius. Removing the cranes created a single, defensible access point against attack from below, the steps, rather than multiple vulnerabilities along the cliff edge. "But why are they so determined to reach the Quay? What's down there?"

Lukkar's shoulders rise and fall in another shrug, this one seeming less certain than dismissive. "Some say there's an ancient temple to their evil gods beneath the falls. Others claim valuable minerals in the cliff face. The people of Swansbane guard whatever secrets they have closely." A wry smile crosses his face. "All I know is the pay's good, and every few months I get to remember what it feels like to put arrows into something that deserves killing."

The admission brings Lukkar's transformed persona into sharper focus. His bow isn't merely decorative, nor his sword simply ornamental. The man enjoys combat, misses it from some earlier occupation, just as Mardonius sometimes finds himself longing for the brutal clarity of battlefield decisions.

"Is that why you hired us?" Mardonius asks. "For the fighting?"

"Partly," Lukkar admits. "The original plan was to find the courier myself. But when Akantha came looking for work, and you showed up with the caravan..." He trails off, gesturing vaguely. "Seemed like a good opportunity for assessment. Master Gynn is always looking for reliable contractors, especially ones with - particular skills."

Something in his tone draws Mardonius' attention. "Assessment?"

"I'm one of two guard commanders at Gynn's Exotic Goods," Lukkar explains with evident pride. "Part of my job is finding talent." He glances sidelong at Mardonius, his expression calculated. "You both performed well. Completed the mission, worked together under pressure despite your differences, showed initiative. The kind of people who might be useful for Master Gynn's more... specialised ventures."

Lukkar's voice drops further, though Akantha remains well ahead of them on her donkey. "The kind of work that keeps a man anonymous, should any people come looking for him."

The implication hangs between them, and Mardonius feels his chest tighten. His initial instinct flares - threat, exposure, danger - before understanding dawns. This isn't a threat, its acknowledgment. Lukkar, and by extension, Master Gynn, knows about his situation with Licarin, the feud that drove him from the Royal City. They know of the powerful enemy who would see him dead rather than accept the truth about his son's death.

Mardonius studies Lukkar's profile, searching for deceit or manipulation and finding only straightforward business calculation. "What sort of specialised ventures?"

In a louder voice to ensure Akantha is party to their conversation he explains, "Retrieval of rare items. Investigation of Ruins. Lots of fun, with plenty of exercise and fresh air to make sure we old warriors don't get too soft." Lukkar's grin returns, sharper now. "Plus, the pay is damned good if you have the stomach for wet-work."

The term lands like a stone in still water, its implications rippling outward. Wet-work: blood work. Tomb raiding and monster hunting perhaps, or something equally morally ambiguous. Yet the prospect of steady employment, of coin enough to eventually buy land far from Licarin's influence, tempts him despite the potential cost to whatever remains of his honour.

The silence that follows feels loaded with unspoken possibilities. Ahead, the forest begins to thin, suggesting they're approaching the halfway point Lukkar mentioned earlier. Akantha glances back looking directly at him, her expression unreadable at this distance, though Mardonius wonders if she too has received some version of this offer.

He considers his current position. Perhaps, like Swansbane, he must adapt to survive.

CHAPTER 14

Aissentur's first hovels appear before them as the last of the light bleeds from the sky, their silhouettes a jagged interruption against the rapidly darkening sky and endless grassy plains. Mardonius shifts his weight, he is sore from a long day on a hard wagon's bench. His body carries the accumulated aches of their journey but strongest of all is the bone-deep weariness that settles into a man's joints after danger has passed but vigilance cannot yet be abandoned.

The locals barely glance at Lukkar's wagon, even though a few nervously avert their eyes from Akantha and her mount. A few torches flare along the town's main thoroughfare, merchants shuttering windows and pulling carts inside for the night. The wagon wheels rattle over cobblestones, each jolt a fresh reminder of bruised muscles.

"Almost there," Lukkar announces, the wagon turning left at The Stuck Elf tavern.

Akantha rides alongside on Ferfer, her posture proud despite the evident fatigue in her eyes. The donkey's hooves clip against stone and it holds itself with surprising dignity, as though full of the pride that comes from bearing a Takaz'Ran warrior.

Not long after, Master Gynn's warehouse looms ahead, a squat fortress of weathered timber rising two stories against the darkened sky. Only a single merchant's sign, generic and faded, hangs above the narrow door. A token gesture that barely distinguishes the building from any common storehouse.

"Not your typical merchant's storefront," Mardonius observes, probing now he understands a little more about their operation here.

"Master Gynn doesn't deal in typical merchandise," Lukkar replies with a wink, easing the wagon into the courtyard fronting the loading doors.

The large doors swing inward before they fully stop, two burly men emerge to take charge of the horses. A third worker approaches the wagon's rear, assessing the valuable timber with a critical eye.

Mardonius dismounts without grace, his stiffened muscles protest the sudden movement, marching may be hard but he thinks he prefers it to a long day seated on a hard board.

The stone courtyard stretches before the warehouse entrance, clean-swept and well-maintained despite the constant traffic of goods. Lanterns hang from iron brackets, their flames protected from the evening breeze by clouded glass, casting pools of amber light that do little to hold back the gathering darkness.

The warehouse interior opens before them as they step through the threshold. A woman approaches from between two tall shelving units, her steps quick and confident. She wears the fitted robes of a professional scribe, hers is dark blue fabric with silver piping at the cuffs and collar, it is practical enough for work but clearly expensive. A wooden tablet hangs from her belt alongside a leather case that likely contains writing implements. Her hair is pulled back severely from a face that shows no sign of welcome.

"You have the case?" she asks without preamble.

The directness catches him off-guard after days of Swansbane's cryptic responses and Lukkar's calculated half-truths. "Yes," he confirms, suddenly hesitant to relinquish the object that has defined their purpose these past days.

"Master Gynn is waiting," she prompts, extending her hand impatiently.

Mardonius reaches beneath his armour, feeling the warm metal against his skin. The case has ridden against his ribs since they left the Fisher Folk lair, a constant presence through combat and conversation. Extracting it creates an odd sense of loss, as though surrendering something that has become part of him. He places it in the scribe's outstretched hand, noting how she immediately examines the seal to ensure it is intact and untampered with.

"Your payment will be confirmed once the contents are verified," she states, tucking the case into a pocket in her robe's sleeves. "Wait in the staff room."

Lukkar claps a hand on Mardonius' shoulder. "Best do as she says, when the boss is watching she is never in the mood for distractions. The kitchen's still serving, so might as well fill your bellies while the scribes do their work." He gestures toward a doorway at the far end of the warehouse floor. "Akantha, you'll want to stable that beast of yours, you know where to take her."

Akantha slides from Ferfer's back with surprising grace for someone who's spent the entire day riding bareback. "Meet you inside," she says to Mardonius, a simple statement that nonetheless marks a shift in their relationship. Mardonius finds himself pleasantly surprised.

As she leads her donkey away, Mardonius takes a moment to fully appreciate where he is.

Workers move past him with sidelong glances, dipping their chins in that particular way men acknowledge each other when they've never met but understand what the other is. Mardonius catches the pattern after the third such interaction. They don't know him, they just know the look of a man who's just completed one of Master Gynn's 'assignments' and lived to collect payment.

He makes his way to the staff room, weaving between stacks of exotic timber and crates marked with symbols from lands he's never visited. His mission complete, his responsibility discharged. In its place, a curious emptiness spreads beneath his ribs, the kind of hollow space that follows purpose fulfilled, waiting to be filled with whatever comes next.

The staff room buzzes with muted conversation, a pocket of warmth and humanity carved from the warehouse's cavernous expanse. Quite some time has passed since their arrival, the wooden bowls before Mardonius and Akantha long scraped clean of a hearty stew that tasted far better than a merchant's backroom had any right to serve. The small hearth under the pot crackles, its flames painting shifting patterns across rough wooden tables where workers pause between tasks to rest, eat, or exchange information in the efficient shorthand of colleagues who need few words to communicate.

Mardonius massages his neck, working through a knot of tension that formed during their journey. The bench beneath him reminds him of how sore he was on the journey back to Aissentur. Across the table, Akantha sits with her back to the wall. They are both struggling with this exercise in patience; eating, resting and waiting for the mysterious scribe to verify their delivery and process their payment.

The warehouse staff moves around them with delicate care, giving Akantha's table a noticeably wider berth than necessary. Their glances slide toward her then jump away, they are not hostile looks, but wary ones. Her Takaz'Ran heritage marks her as different in a town where difference often means danger. She bears their scrutiny with aloof indifference, her posture neither inviting approach nor challenging observation.

A broad-shouldered man carrying a stack of wax tablets veers his path to avoid passing directly past her, though plenty of space exists. These small exclusions accumulate like grains of sand, individually insignificant but collectively unmistakable.

"Always like this?" Mardonius asks, keeping his voice low.

Akantha's mouth quirks into a quick sly smile. "Takaz'Ran not welcome in polite houses." She sips from her cup, eyes tracking movement across the room. "Used to it. Good for all to know their place."

He understands the dynamics at play. She is not the only one being put in their place by this charade, their fear marks them too. Outsiders face suspicion everywhere, but he imagines the Takaz'Ran carry additional burdens with their fierce independence often misinterpreted as hostility. He guessed their tribal ways are viewed as primitive by town-dwellers who've never witnessed their skill in battle or the social structures that bind their tribe with the closeness of a single family.

The door swings open, admitting Lukkar. His transformation is absolute now. He wears a simple tunic and leather pants, they are well-made but deliberately understated, his weapons are absent but their ghostly presence suggested in how he moves, always leaving space at his hip where a sword would hang.

Lukkar ladles stew from the communal pot into a wooden bowl, exchanges brief words with a worker, then turns to survey the room. His gaze falls on Mardonius and Akantha and offers them a subtle wink before crossing to their table.

"Mind if I join you?" he asks, already settling onto the bench beside Mardonius. "Been a long day."

The effect of his arrival ripples through the common room. Workers who previously avoided their table now glance over with reassessed interest. A young man distributing bread makes his way toward them, offering the basket in a gesture of careful hospitality. Lukkar's acceptance acts as a form of currency in this closed economy of trust.

"Still waiting on the quill warriors?" Lukkar asks around a mouthful of stew.

"Seems they're thorough," Mardonius replies.

"That they are. Master Gynn doesn't rush verification." Lukkar tears off a chunk of bread. "Be worth the wait, though."

They eat their bread in companionable silence for several minutes, the background noise of the warehouse, creaking floorboards, shifting crates, muted conversations, forming a constant undercurrent to their rest. Eventually, Lukkar excuses himself to speak with a foreman, leaving them alone again.

"Your arm," Mardonius says, looking toward the bruise visible beneath Akantha's bandages. "How is it?"

She extends her arm on the table between them, allowing him to examine the injury he'd tended last night. The bruise has evolved into a landscape of purple and yellow, its edges fading into her skin. He gently probes the area, feeling for heat or swelling that might indicate complications.

"Tender?" he asks.

"Manageable."

His fingers trace the edge of the discoloration, noting how she doesn't flinch from his touch as she might have only last night. Their shared battle at Swansbane has further lowered the barriers between them.

He takes his time replenishing the poultice on her arm before carefully rewrapping the bandage.

"Should heal clean," he concludes, sitting back. "Might want fresh herbs in a day or two."

Akantha rolls her arm to ensure freedom of movement. "What you think of Lukkar's offer?" she asks, changing the subject with characteristic directness.

Mardonius considers the question, aware this conversation has been brewing since the Swansbane road. "More work means more coin," he says carefully. "And Master Gynn seems to value discretion."

"Good for you," she observes, the statement carrying multiple layers of meaning.

Good for a man hiding from powerful enemies.

Good for someone needing to rebuild resources quickly.

"Good for both of us," he counters, "if you're interested."

She studies him, weighing something behind those guarded eyes. "Fought well together on wall," she says finally. "You see the mage-threat fast. I take down the big warriors." A pause. "Balanced skills."

The assessment is objective, yet Mardonius feels a warmth at this acknowledgment of their compatibility in battle. If he has learned anything from her, it is that this is the highest praise a Takaz'Ran warrior might offer. The direct recognition of mutual value without any emotional embellishment.

"We did," he agrees. "Though I hope the next job involves fewer Twisted and more sleep."

A flicker of amusement crosses her face, not quite a smile, but close enough to count it as a win. "Sleep is overrated."

Around them, the atmosphere in the common room has subtly shifted. A worker delivering kindling for the hearth nods to Akantha as he passes. Another refills their water cups without being asked. These small inclusions balance earlier exclusions, tentative acceptance extended through minor gestures.

Returning briefly to the room, Lukkar glances their way, satisfaction evident in his expression. He's planned this, Mardonius realises; placing them in the common room rather than a private office, joining them publicly, leaving them to be observed by the warehouse staff. It is a considered process of integration, establishing them as affiliated with Master Gynn's operation rather than a disposable hired hands.

Mardonius stretches his legs beneath the table, feeling the pleasant ache of muscles finally allowed to rest. Their mission is complete, their partnership technically concluded. Yet here they sit, discussing future possibilities as though continuation is assumed rather than negotiated.

"If the pay's good," Akantha says, returning to the question of further work, "and is honest work..." She stops herself, amending: "Honourable, at least. I would say yes."

"Good," Mardonius responds, surprised by how much her answer pleases him. "I would too."

Outside, night has fully claimed Aissentur. Inside this warm room, surrounded by the mechanics of commerce and the subtle currents of social hierarchy, they've found an unexpected pocket of potential. It may not be not be safety exactly, but perhaps it is the nearest approximation for two people carrying so many burdens from their pasts.

The scribe's footsteps announce her return, a soft tread on the wooden floor that nevertheless cuts through the common room's ambient noise. Mardonius straightens, pushing away the fog of fatigue that had begun to settle over him during their wait. Each step echoes with the sound of someone whose time is precisely accounted for. The workers nearest the doorway acknowledge her with deferential half-bows as she passes, her blue robes swaying with her stride as she approaches their table directly.

The lamplight catches the silver threads woven through her collar as she stops before them, her posture impeccable despite the late hour. No hint of warmth softens her professional demeanour, yet neither does any disdain colour her assessment of the two tired and road-worn mercenaries seated before her. She places a small wooden tray on the table between them.

"Your payment." she announces, "Two silver coins each, as contracted."

The coins catch the flickering light as they rest in their separate depressions on the tray. Four silver discs, their edges worn smooth from circulation, their faces stamped with the profile of the current Ran on one side and Eanna on the other. More wealth than Mardonius has held at any one time since fleeing the Royal City.

"Master Gynn confirms the contract is complete and correctly executed," the scribe continues, producing a small scroll from within her robe. She unwinds it fully and lays it on the table, turning it toward them. "Your marks, please, confirming receipt of payment."

Mardonius presses his thumb to the offered ink pad beside the scroll before making his mark next to his name. The act feels strangely formal after days of life-or-death struggles in tunnels and on walls. Akantha follows suit, her thumb print appearing below his in the neat column of recipient acknowledgments.

The scribe waits until the ink dries before rolling the paper and secreting it away in her sleeve. "The mission parameters have been satisfied, and all obligations discharged." Her formulaic words carry the weight of contractual closure.

Mardonius reaches for his coins, the metal cool against his palm as he slides them into his pouch. He mentally calculates his current holdings: four silver coins with half of that from this job, two coppers, and nineteen bits rounding that out. Enough to live modestly for a month or two without work. Enough to top up his depleted healing pouch and grab some necessities. Not enough for land or security, but far from the desperate poverty that had dogged him since his disgrace.

A small victory, but victories have been rare enough lately that he savours this one fully.

Across the table, Akantha tucks her coins away, her expression betraying nothing of what this payment might mean to her ambitions. Two silver coins buys no war horse, but its two coins closer to her dream than she was yesterday.

The scribe remains standing, her task apparently not yet complete. "Master Gynn wishes to know if you would be interested in additional contracted work," she says, her tone giving no indication of her own opinion on the matter. "Similar parameters with appropriate compensation."

Mardonius hesitates, considering. The brass case is delivered, their obligation fulfilled. They could part ways now, each following their separate paths with pockets heavier than before. The sensible choice would be to move on, avoid forming connections that might complicate his need for anonymity.

He glances at Akantha, expecting indifference or perhaps the same pragmatic evaluation he feels. Instead, he finds her eyes already on him, something unexpected in her expression. She holds his look for a measured moment, then offers a small but definite nod, agreement, perhaps even encouragement.

The gesture surprises him more than any danger they've faced together. This proud Takaz'Ran warrior, who initially regarded him with barely concealed disdain, now volunteering to extend their partnership.

"Yes," he tells the scribe, still looking at Akantha. "We're interested."

Something flickers across the scribe's composed features, it could be satisfaction or perhaps just simple confirmation of an expected outcome. "Master Gynn will be pleased. You are offered lodging for the night. Further details will follow in the morning."

"Lodging sounds good," Mardonius says, exhaustion making him incautious. "I speak from experience when I say the floors are comfortable here."

His attempt at humour slides off the scribe's professional demeanour like water from oiled leather. She regards him with the same emotion she might direct at a shipping manifest. "The sleeping quarters are adequate. Please remain here. Someone will attend you shortly." With that, she turns and departs, her footsteps fading into the background noise of the warehouse.

"Not one for jokes," Mardonius mutters, embarrassment warming his face.

Akantha shrugs, the ghost of amusement in her eyes. "Big chief," she offers as though this explains everything.

The common room gradually empties as workers finish their meals and return to tasks or depart for the night. The hearth fire burns lower, casting longer shadows across the wooden tables. Mardonius finds himself fighting a losing battle against fatigue, his eyes growing heavier with each passing moment. The past days have demanded more than his body wants to give and now, with danger temporarily abated and payment secured, exhaustion claims its due.

He catches himself drifting off, his head jerking up suddenly when the warehouse door opens, admitting a blast of cooler night air. Not Lukkar. Just workers changing shifts. His eyes drift closed again despite his efforts, the surrounding sounds blending into a soothing backdrop.

Mardonius forces himself awake, focusing on the grain patterns in the wooden table to maintain consciousness. The room wavers slightly, his vision blurring at the edges. When had he last truly slept? Before Swansbane certainly. Before the Fisher Folk and their underwater lair. His mind drifts. Mission complete. Contract fulfilled. The thoughts circle like lazy birds, never quite landing.

Another door opens. He straightens, blinking hard. Not Lukkar. His head droops forward again, chin nearly touching his chest before he jerks upright. Across the table, Akantha watches him with what might be amusement or concern, his exhaustion makes reading expressions difficult.

"Rest," she says. "I watch."

The simple offer touches something deep in his soldier's heart. The fundamental trust of comrades who guard each other's sleep in dangerous places. He wants to thank her, but exhaustion slurs his thoughts before they reach his tongue. Instead, he attempts a grateful wave before his eyelids betray him once more.

Most of the workers are gone, the remaining few moving with the slowness of a shift nearing its end. Lukkar grabs a three-legged stool from beside the hearth, dragging it across the floor with a scrape that jolts Mardonius fully awake. The guard commander, looks fresher than he has any right to be after their journey, his face washed clean and eyes bright.

"Apologies for the wait," Lukkar says, setting his stool at the end of their table. "Matters required the Master's personal attention."

The common room feels larger now that it's emptier. Night sounds filter through the walls: distant shouts from the street, the occasional rattle of a passing cart, the soft hooting of an owl that has made its home somewhere in the warehouse eaves. The fire has burned down to a solid core of embers, its light more suggestion than illumination.

"The scroll was intact," Lukkar continues, leaning forward with forearms braced against the table. "In perfect condition, in fact. Exactly as we'd hoped." He scratches his chin, freshly shaved but already showing stubble. "Unfortunately, no one here can read it."

Mardonius frowns, forcing his tired mind to focus. "Not readable? All that for nothing?"

"Oh, it's readable all right. Just not by us." Lukkar's mouth twists into a grimace as he taps the table with two fingers. "Old Chilissar script. Might as well be fish tracks in mud to most folk." He leans forward, lowering his voice. "Master Gynn needs it taken to a specialist. Man lives less than a day's ride from here, but he's..." Lukkar's eyes narrow, searching for the right word. "Let's just say he doesn't welcome most visitors."

"Why us?" Mardonius asks, professional caution cutting through his fatigue. "Surely Master Gynn has regular couriers."

Lukkar's eyes crinkle with approval at the question. "He does. But this particular translator refuses to deal with most of us locals. Bad blood, not letting bygones be bygones and all that." He waves his hand dismissively. "Fresh faces have better chances. Plus, you've proven you can handle yourselves if complications arise."

"Name the translator," Akantha says suddenly, her first direct question to Lukkar all evening.

"Details tomorrow," Lukkar continues. "Who, what, where and how much. You are not beholden until you know the full story."

"We're interested," Mardonius says, glancing at Akantha for confirmation. She tilts her head in cautious agreeance.

"Excellent." Lukkar stands, stretching his back with a series of audible pops. "Rest well tonight. You'll want to be fresh in the morning." He gestures toward the rear area of the warehouse. "Sleeping quarters through there. Nothing fancy, but the rooms are clean, vermin free and there's even a bit of warm water put out for washing."

They rise from the table, Mardonius' muscles protesting the movement after too long sitting on yet another hard bench. Fatigue weighs on him like wet wool, his limbs heavy and uncooperative. He follows Lukkar through the doorway into the warehouse and thence a narrow hallway lined with small chambers. This time he is allocated a modest, but private, sleeping room, one probably offered to trusted traders who need to stay overnight.

"That one's yours," Lukkar says to Akantha, pointing to a door on the left. "Wash basin inside, fresh drying cloth on the shelf if you want it." She disappearing inside without further comment.

Lukkar gestures Mardonius toward the next door, but before he can enter the guard commander catches his arm. The grip is light but intentional, a fellow soldier's request for momentary attention. He lowers his voice, though no one remains in the hallway.

"Word came in while you were waiting, it's why we took so long to get back to you." Lukkar says, eyes suddenly serious beneath his perpetually smiling brows. "Scouts have been checking inns and villages along The Mountain Way. They're asking questions about former soldiers, specifically ones of your rank."

Mardonius feels a cold weight settle in his stomach, fatigue instantly burning away. "Licarin," he says, the name bitter on his tongue.

"Seems likely. They're traveling methodically, expected in Aissentur within two days." Lukkar releases his arm, his expression neutral but his meaning clear. "This trip east puts you out of their path. By the time you return, they should have moved on."

The warning is a gift, valuable information freely given when it could have been withheld. Mardonius recognises it for what it is: trust extended, circumstantial protection offered. Not from obligation or contract, but from one veteran to another.

"I appreciate the heads-up," Mardonius says, the inadequate words carrying more weight than they can properly bear.

Lukkar waves away the thanks with a warrior's discomfort at sentiment. "We can sort out the details tomorrow. For now, sleep. You look like something even the Twisted would refuse to eat."

The crude humour breaks the tension, allowing them both retreat from the uncomfortable territory of gratitude. Mardonius feels an unexpected connection to this man who has dropped his deceptions and offered genuine assistance.

Lukkar turns to leave, but before he takes a step, Mardonius' arm moves of its own accord. His right fist strikes his left breast in the formal salute of the Eastern Legion.

Lukkar freezes for a heartbeat, surprise flickering across his features. Then, with precise movements that speak of years of drilling, he returns the gesture.

No words pass between them. None are needed. The exchange confirms what Mardonius had begun to suspect, Lukkar too had served, perhaps even in the same legion. The salutes acknowledge a bond that transcends their current circumstances, a shared language of duty and sacrifice that civilians can never fully comprehend.

Lukkar departs, his footsteps fading into the ambient creaking of the ancient warehouse. Mardonius enters his assigned room, finding a narrow pallet that looks more inviting than any feather bed simply because it offers the promise of uninterrupted rest.

He manages to remove his boots and outer leather armour before exhaustion claims its victory. As he stretches out on the pallet, the events of the past days shuffle through his mind like badly dealt cards. Fisher Folk, brass case, Swansbane's walls, Twisted attacks, silver coins, Licarin's spies. The images blur and overlap, losing coherence as sleep rushes in to claim him.

Then darkness takes him, deep and dreamless. The sleep of a soldier who knows that someone trustworthy stands the watch.

ABOUT THE AUTHOR

S. K. Moonie

S. K. Moonie. The name was as strange as any Mardonius had encountered, but perhaps it suited the kind of mind that would imagine a world like this. A world where kindness was brittle and justice, like the light at dawn, only touched the highest places and never lingered long on the ground. All through the long, blue-shadowed march from his homeland to the fetid edges of the world, Mardonius had been haunted not by the faces of friends lost to the sword or the screams of dying horses, but by the sense that someone, somewhere, had set these trials in his path for their own private amusement. This S. K. Moonie, it seemed, was just such a person: not a god, nor a demon, but an author, a craftsman of suffering who delighted in chaining men to their worst instincts and then watching them gnaw off their own limbs.

He learned from his fellow officers, between sips of watered ale, that Moonie was an Australian of all things. A race of men supposedly given over to salt air, strong drink, and the stubbornness born of living on an island stolen by convicts. Perhaps this explained the relentless bleakness of the tales spun about the world: none of the victories lasted, every virtue was a finite resource and the roads were always running endlessly before you.

The first book, 'Forsaken Road,' they said, had been blocked out and all but completed years ago. It was only now, after some lengthy absence or reversal of fortune, had Moonie found the time or the will to polish the story for publication.

Mardonius felt an odd kinship toward this invisible author, sensing in the man's labour a kind of mirrored anguish. Like himself, Moonie had once believed there was a logic to the world, a lawfulness that, while sometimes cruel, was at least consistent. But reality was always more complicated: supplies ran out, men deserted, and sometimes the people you trusted most stuck a knife in your back. Gritty, they called it. Dark Fantasy, as if that phrase could encompass the taste of mud in your teeth, or the oily stink of fear that rose from a camp about to be overrun. In this world, the heroes were not always right because there was rarely a right to be found, just a thousand tiny wrongs, each waiting their turn in the dark.

What Moonie seemed to prize above all, Mardonius observed, was the struggle itself: not the clean fairy-tale struggle between good and evil, but the endless, grinding fight against hunger, mistrust, and the small indignities that hollowed out a soul. Characters were not born for glory but for endurance. Poverty was no abstraction but a daily knotted stomach. Bigotry was a force as constant as the wind across the plains. You could not talk your way out of these things. You could only lean into the pain and hope that, at the end of the grind, the person left standing was still recognisably yourself.

So Mardonius marched on, his own story tangled in Moonie's web, wondering how much of himself would remain when the telling was done. He did not know if his fate would be to die in a ditch. Perhaps he would be fortunate enough to find some fleeting peace, instead of becoming just another punctuation mark in the endless, pitiless histories of men. All he knew was that, in this world, the only certainty was that nothing came without cost and that some stories could only be written in scars.

BOOKS IN THIS SERIES

The War for Swansbane